THE
Kano,
THE
Teacher
& THE
# Lola

A FILIPINO-AMERICAN FABLE

THE
Kano,
THE
Teacher
& THE
Lola

A FILIPINO-AMERICAN FABLE

CHRISTOPHER HOLL

A. J. NEAL
PUBLISHING

A. J. NEAL
P U B L I S H I N G

Published by A.J. Neal Publishing
915 Bennetts Mills Road #1469
Jackson, NJ 08527

Illustrations: Jocelyn Diaz
Copyediting: Lynette M. Smith
Cover design and interior layout: Monkey C Media, monkeyCmedia.com

Banaue Rice Terraces photo:
http://en.wikipedia.org/wiki/Image:Pana_Banaue_Rice_Terraces.JPG

Hardcover print edition ISBN: 978-0-9851442-7-2
Softcover print edition ISBN: 978-0-9851442-8-9
Electronic edition ISBN: 978-0-9851442-9-6

First Printing 2018
Printed in the United States of America
Library of Congress Control Number: 2018907084

10% of the profit from every book sold will be donated to Mary Queen of Heaven Missionaries, Lawaan Talisay City, Cebu, Philippines 6054, https://www.mqhm.org/

To Guillerma F. Amper, the inspiration for this book

Always in Our Hearts

CONTENTS

PROLOGUE

Over three million Filipinos (first and second generation) live in the United States today. Tagalog, the national language of the Philippines, is the fourth most widely spoken foreign language in the US. Filipino-Americans have a median income almost 50 percent higher than US households in general, have a higher education rate compared to native-born citizens, and are much more likely to be naturalized US citizens than immigrants overall.

Three main waves characterize the history of Filipino immigration to the United States: First, students and agricultural workers following the US annexation of the Philippines in 1899; second, military recruits, war brides, and nurses after World War II; and third, families and higher-educated professionals after 1965. Additionally, there is evidence to suggest that as early as the 1700s, Filipino immigrants had found their way to America.

It is the third wave of Filipino immigration that is so personal for me, as this was when my wife and her family came to the United States, around 1980. Theirs is the iconic story of the American Dream—struggle, success, prosperity.

I'm a *kano* (Amerikano) and, though not Filipino by birth, like to think of myself as Filipino in spirit—as evidenced by 28 years of marriage to my *asawa* (spouse/wife), our four "Fil-Am" children, and my love and appreciation for the culture. Over the years, I've become accustomed to certain Filipino practices and various expressions and superstitions, many of which were shared by my mother-in-law. Because I've always enjoyed them, I thought they would make for a great book aimed at the non-Filipino like me, who is interested in the culture or perhaps is dating or marrying a Filipino. Long story short, that's where this book started. But over time, as I wrote and researched, it grew into one geared more for Pinoys themselves, although the original premise is still germane. The subtitle, "A Filipino-American Fable," is a fable only in the whimsical, creative envelope used to deliver on the content, which is based in facts, traditions, and beliefs.

You may have had the experience of hosting out-of-town family or friends, and taking them sightseeing to local landmarks. It isn't unusual that what's old seems new, or at least renewed, through the lens of someone else; or that another's take on something may help you appreciate it a little bit more, if only because you haven't thought much about it. For the Filipino reader, you don't need me to teach you about your culture, but I hope my perspective and appreciation for it adds to, or at least reminds you, of what you already know and love about it. For the non-Filipino reader, I hope this book interests you enough to begin your exploration of the culture. Believe me, a treasure trove awaits your discovery.

A word of caution is in order before you begin reading. A central figure in the book is the *Lola*, or Grandmother, who is the guardian of Filipino tradition, folklore, and superstition. In this sense, she is very real. However, to keep the story amusing and engaging, her character is a bit exaggerated and a little "over the top" at times. If humor comes from how creatively we're able to stretch the truth without going too far—hopefully, I've stopped just in time!

It's said that when you marry a Filipina, you marry her whole family. Thank goodness, as every one of my *pamilya* has been a tremendous blessing in my life—and, without whom (along with my wife, of course!) this volume could not have been written.

I hope you enjoy the book. *Umaasa ako na gusto mo ang libro.*

CHAPTER 1

WAX ON, WAX OFF

With his head buried in the palms of his hands, the young man sat slumped over his kitchen table, replaying in his mind the awful afternoon that had taken place a few hours earlier. "Ahh, why was I such a fool?" he asked himself.

Only it wasn't to himself.

Suddenly, a figure appeared in the kitchen before him, and said, "I picked up on your thought waves, and sensed you are troubled."

"Hey, how did you get in here?"

"Do not be frightened; I am here to help you. I know why you are so distraught."

"How would you know anything about me—and hey, why am I even talking to you? Now, get out of here before I call the police!"

"Please, don't do that. You are embarrassed and ashamed because you did not act so thoughtfully at your girlfriend's party, did you?"

"Wait. How can you know that? Who are you? Oh my gosh. You're a ghost, you're a ghost! Aah!"

"Please, I'm not a ghost. Not even close. Think of me as your Teacher."

"My teacher? I don't need a teacher. I've got a college degree… and an MBA."

"And think of yourself as the *Kano*."

"What?" he said. "The kah-know?"

"Yes, the Kano. And it sounds just like you said it—kah-know. I am the Teacher, and you are the Kano."

"Hello? My name is Michael. And what can you possibly teach me?" he asked.

"The Way of the Filipino. So that you may get to know this girl better."

"Okay, this is getting weird. How do you know that my girlfriend is Filipino?"

"She is Filipina," corrected the Teacher.

"That's what I said, Filipino."

"Technically, you are correct," said the Teacher. "She is a Filipino."

The young man, happy with himself, said, "Hmm. Glad you agree with me… *Teacher*."

"Now, tell me about this party and why you are so troubled and unhappy."

"Well," he began, "I kind of laughed at my girlfriend's family… uh, hopefully future girlfriend's family, and her customs… and the way they were speaking. Are you sure you're not a ghost?"

"I'm sure. Now, that doesn't sound too promising," said the Teacher. "Let's start at the beginning. Tell me about this girl."

"Well, she's beautiful. She was born in the Philippines, came to the US a few years ago, and recently became a naturalized citizen."

"That's nice to hear. Let me guess—she's a nurse," said the Teacher.

"How did you know?"

"And her name is Maria," he continued.

"Y-yes…. Hey, who—or what—are you, anyway?"

"Like I said, I am here to teach you The Way of the Filipino," said the Teacher. "It's not uncommon for a kano to really mess things up in the beginning. Especially at a party—where for the first time in your life you may see fish served with the head still on—and, oh, those little black eyes staring right at you."

"Yes," said the Kano. "It was like that exactly. Those eyes seemed to follow me around the table. And then there was the chocolate pudding, which wasn't served with the other desserts. It was placed with the entrees. That was odd, but even stranger was when everyone was whispering and giggling as I scooped some of the chocolate pudding on my plate—like there was a secret or something going on."

"I'll explain the chocolate pudding thing later. Now, how long has Maria been your girlfriend?" asked the Teacher.

"Well, admittedly, she's not my girlfriend—yet. I want her to be. Right now, she just thinks of me as a friend."

"A friend? You? Someone who doesn't appreciate her culture? Then why would you want to be her boyfriend?"

"She's soooo beautiful!"

"Yes, that goes without saying. The Filipina is extraordinarily beautiful. A mix of Malay, Chinese, and Spanish—she's the most beautiful woman in the world, really. No one can hold a candle to her. Unless it's another Filipina doing the candle dance, but that's another story."

"The candle dance?"

"Yes, it's called the *pandanggo sa ilaw*, and it's a Philippine folk dance, which, while graceful, is hard to perform, because the dancers balance oil lamps on their heads and on the back of their hands. Now, tell me what else you did wrong."

"I was having a hard time following some conversation, especially with her older relatives. For instance, I was listening to one of her aunts tell a story, and at first, it seemed to be about a high school boy and his soccer game, as her aunt used the pronoun *he* when describing the boy's kicking ability; but as she continued the story, the pronoun changed to *she*, so I thought maybe I missed something, like there was a girl in the story too—but then her aunt switched the pronoun back to *he*, and then back to *she*, but the story was still just about the boy, and well… I felt like I was watching a tennis match with all the back and forth of the *he's* and *she's!*"

"'He said, she said,' is more than just an American expression… for the Filipino, it's reflective of their native language not having such a distinction in gender," said the Teacher. "You may have heard the word *siya* spoken, which means either *he* or *she*. So be sensitive to that. Over time, you won't even notice. What else happened?"

"I laughed at some things that were said…. I guess they were superstitions," said the Kano.

"Like what?"

"Well, her grandmother—I think she called her *Lolo* and—"

"*Lola*," the Teacher interrupted. "With an *a* at the end. Lol*a*. Lolo, with an *o*, would be Grandfather."

"Yeah. Anyway, when Maria scratched her nose, her grandmother, I mean her lola, said it meant that someone was kissing her picture. It was harmless enough, but I laughed in a smug, sort of 'I know better than you' kind of way.

Maria asked me why I was laughing. 'What a silly belief,' I told her."

"How did that go over?"

"She seemed a little offended," said the Kano. "Maybe she thought I was insulting her lola."

"What happened next?"

"I was a bit stand-offish about some of the other dishes. There was some kind of meaty-tomato saucy vegetable thing called *menudo*. I couldn't help but laugh at the name, because it was the same as that 1980s Latin boy band called Menudo, and I joked that anyone over 15 shouldn't be allowed to eat the dish, just like how a member of the group was kicked out once they turned 15."

"And how did that go over with Maria's family?"

"Probably would have been better had I not been so dismissive earlier," said the Kano. "But," he continued, "the icing on the cake was when they brought out the karaoke machine."

"Why? Did you sing 'My Way' badly?" asked the Teacher with a laugh.

"No, I said I hated karaoke, and that only people who can't sing like to use the machine. Instantly, a loud *haa* rang out! Actually, it was more like a long, shrieky *haaaaa*! Then, the room went silent. You could have heard a pin drop. Everybody was staring at me. Everybody. Like I had committed a grand offense," said the Kano. "Then, I saw some people raising their eyebrows at me, while their heads sort of leaned back. It was like they were communicating to each other in silence, using only their eyebrows."

"I see," said the Teacher.

"What's with the eyebrows?" asked the Kano. "You know, the moving up and down, I saw a lot of that. Anyway, they seemed insulted, for reasons I don't know."

"Think of it as eyebrow talk, Kano. Two things you need to be conscious of. Filipinos greet each other with their eyebrows. First there's eye contact, then both eyebrows are raised up and brought down. It's accompanied by a smile, of course, and it's a way to say hello without speaking a word."

"Okay, fine. I did see some of that. But when I made the remark about the karaoke, I didn't notice any smiles."

"Yes, in that case, you saw her family and guests give you a backward toss of their heads accompanied by some hard eye contact," said the Teacher.

"Yes, that was it exactly."

"That signals a bit of a challenge, a bit of push-back."

"Well, I didn't mean any harm."

"Kano, you insulted Maria's family and friends. Karaoke is a beloved pastime among Filipinos. How could you say they all had bad voices?"

"I didn't say they *all* had bad voices."

"You need to drop your attitude of superiority, Kano. First, because you are not superior. Second, because you want to get Maria back. Isn't that right?"

"Yes, that's right."

"Did you know," said the Teacher, "That karaoke was invented by a Filipino?"

"Uh, no, I didn't know that."

"Yes, it's true. Roberto Del Rosario invented what he called the Sing Along System in 1974. It's still what you see today—a portable device with a microphone and amplifier that produces a multitude of musical sound effects. And yes, it can enhance one's voice too."

"Sing Along System? Is that the same as karaoke?" asked the Kano.

"Yes, one and the same. It became better known as karaoke by its Japanese pirates, but, it's still the same system Del Rosario invented. He patented over 20 other acoustic inventions, including the OMB or One Man Band."

"Interesting," said the Kano. "I'll be sure to impress Maria with my knowledge of her people."

"Not so fast, Kano, one fun fact does not make you an expert. Besides knowing about a few things, more important is knowing—that you want to sincerely know more about the Filipino culture."

"Yes, I do know that I want to know more about the Filipino culture, Teacher. And to get to know Maria better. So she won't say no to me. You know?"

"Where do things stand between you and Maria know? I mean now. Where are things now?" asked the Teacher.

"After an awkward departure from the party, I texted her that evening. No response. Called twice the next day. No response. I think I've really blown it."

"Kano, I think you care about this girl, beyond her obvious beauty. You regret your behavior, because aside from being rude and boorish, you've come to realize that Maria and her Filipino culture don't come a la carte or even Chinese menu style, where you select one part of her culture from column A, another from column B. She's a package deal, right from the start."

"Yes, I think you're right."

"What you need," said the Teacher, "is a guide—a teacher. You need instruction and training in The Way of the Filipino. That's the only way you'll get back Maria. I can be the teacher you need. Are you interested? Are you in?"

"Am I in? Does Filipino chocolate pudding taste like... er, I won't go there. Yes, I'm in!"

"Then it is settled. And, you must remember, Kano, there is no turning back. It's like having an amazing Jollibee Yum Burger. Once you've tasted it, it's what everything else is compared to. Are you sure you're ready?"

"Jollibee? Uh, yeah, sure—yes, I'm ready. What's next?"

With that, the Teacher extended his right arm towards the young man, holding out his hand, fist closed, palm up.

"Look," said the Teacher.

The Kano's eyes were fixated as the Teacher slowly uncurled his fingers, exposing something in his hand— it appeared to be a fried food, light brown in color and tubular in shape. Curiously, background music, like that in a martial arts movie when the student learns from the master, began to fill the room.

"*Pagbabagong-anyo*," said the Teacher.

"Ga-gong? Pag a what? Banyo? Isn't that a bathroom? What are you saying? Do you need to use the restroom?"

"Kano, pagbabagong-anyo is Tagalog for 'transformation.' In order to win Maria's heart, you need to be transformed."

"Transformed? What's wrong with me now? To quote Popeye, 'I yam who I yam.'"

"And how far has that gotten you? Kano, to win Maria's heart, you need to become a beautiful butterfly, like the Magellan birdwing, instead of the coarse moth you are today."

"Moths are *so* underappreciated."

"Now, back to what I'm holding. This *lumpia shanghai* represents—"

"What? Shanghai? Isn't that in China?" interrupted the Kano. "Maria's from the Philippines. And, I don't think that brown thing looks lumpy, it looks pretty smooth. Except that one area near your thumb, which is a bit crushed—did you smoosh that lumpy Chinese thing you're holding, Teacher?"

"Kano, it's called lumpia shanghai, and if you'd like, think of it as a Filipino spring roll. It's a delicious delicacy, but for your training, it will represent your transformation."

"Teacher, I'm not following you."

"Your transformation. To become a Filipino in spirit, like me—just like me. And have a chance to win Maria back."

"Like you? Um, don't take this the wrong way, Teacher, but, you know, I'm not all that interested in poofing into people's lives out of nowhere. And, well, I'm also quite a bit younger than you."

"You want to win Maria's heart, isn't that right?"

"Of course."

"Then, by way of instruction and training, you will begin your transformation in The Way of the Filipino. As you acquire the requisite knowledge and wisdom, I will give you a lumpia shanghai. It will signify that you have gained a greater understanding and appreciation for the Filipino culture, and have taken a step forward in your transformation."

"Does this mean there's going to be tests? I'm not a good test-taker, Teacher. Will it be multiple choice? What if I mark *C* as the answer too often?"

"No tests, just lumpia shanghai."

"Okay, but what do I do with it?"

"You eat it."

"Eat it?"

"Yes."

"Hmm, this is my kind of training. Can there be lots of transformations? Those lumpy Chinese things smell pretty good."

"They're lumpia! But, when your transformation is almost complete, I won't be giving you a lumpia shanghai."

"You won't? Are you going to eat it? Teacher, that doesn't seem fair, seeing that I'm doing all the work around here."

"When we reach that stage, Kano, it's all on you. I will not only give you a lumpia, I will…"

"What? What will you do, Teacher?"

"It's not what I will do. It's what you will do. You will take the lumpia shanghai from my hand, because then it will be time for you to—"

"Go?" interrupted the Kano excitedly. "It will be time for me to go? Like Grasshopper, in the movie Kung-Fu? Oh, Teacher, you're so corny."

"No, it won't be time for you to go. It will be time for you to *mano-po*."

"Mah-no? Mah-no who? That Filipino boxer? Mah-know-pack-e-yoh? Teacher, I'm not following you."

"His name is not Mah-know-pack-e-yoh! It's Manny Paquaio, one of the greatest fighters in boxing history! He is the only eight-division world champion, and considered by many, pound for pound, to be the best boxer ever."

"Do you mean that he is considered by *manny* to be the best boxer ever? Get it? Manny? Uh, Teacher, get it? Not many, but Manny?"

"Kano, you have so much to learn… and I have so much to teach you… and there are only 24 hours in the day. Uy!"

Their journey was about to begin.

CHAPTER 2
BREAKFAST AT TIPPANY'S

The next day, at 5 a.m., the alarm clock started buzzing loudly. The young man, disoriented, slapped for the snooze button to stop the relentless, pulsating blast.

"Where am I?" he thought. "Why is my alarm clock set for 5 a.m.?"

"Because that's what I set it for. Time to rise and shine, Kano, rise and shine," said the Teacher as he pulled the covers off the Kano. "Your instruction, your training, has begun."

Grabbing the covers back and pulling them over his head, the Kano grumbled, "I'm only dreaming.... This is just a dream... just a dream... just a..."

"If your dream is to get Maria back, and you're not serious about your training in The Way of the Filipino, then this won't be a dream; it will be your worst nightmare!"

Coming to consciousness, the Kano sat up in bed, stretched, and sniffed. "What's that smell?" he asked.

"Your breakfast. We're eating Filipino this morning."

"Eating Filipinos? You mean they're cannibals? *Aah*!"

"Kano, please. They're not cannibals. What's wrong with you? We're eating Filipino food this morning."

"Smells pretty good," said the Kano. "Mmm, I think I'm getting very hungry now." He put on his robe, walked out the bedroom, and followed the Teacher downstairs. It was dark, except for the light coming from the kitchen. As they entered, the Teacher signaled to the Kano to sit down at the table, and his sleepy eyes widened considerably as he looked upon the kitchen table. "Wow, this is a lot of food!"

"I've been busy cooking, that's for sure," said the Teacher.

"Don't tell me a Filipino eats this much for breakfast every morning—there must be seven or eight dishes here."

"No, Filipinos wouldn't eat all of this at one time," said the Teacher. "But, I want to give you a range of options."

"It really does smell good. Can you describe what we've got here?" asked the Kano.

"Sure." Pointing to the white bowl of rice, the Teacher said, "This one is *sinangag*. It's made from leftover rice, fried up in oil and garlic. This goes great with the plate next to it, and that's *tocino*, or sweetened pork strip."

"Looks good. And what about that one; is that another rice dish?" asked the Kano, pointing to the bowl at the end of the table.

"Yes. This one is white rice, with fried eggs and Spam," said the Teacher.

"Spam? Filipinos like Spam? What about green eggs? Do Filipinos like green eggs and Spam?"

"Manny like Spam. Uh, I mean many like Spam. And corned beef hash, with sautéed onions. I made some of that as well," said the Teacher. "We're talking comfort food here!"

"Hmm," said the Kano as he dug into the sinangag, "this is good." Looking over the table, he asked, "Are those mini hot dogs?"

"Vienna sausages," said the Teacher. "Before meeting my wife, I did not eat these, but when you fry them up with a little butter or oil and serve with rice—wow, really good."

Taking a bite from a small bun, the Kano's eyes widened as big as a lizard's. "Mmm, this is great; what is it?"

"*Pandesal.* So good. It's a small bread bun," said the Teacher. "I warmed them up and put on some butter."

"This is amazing," said the Kano as he bit into the warm, moist, heavenly tasting bun.

"Here try this. It's called *longanisa*," said the Teacher.

Biting into it, the Kano said, "Mmm, this is great too. Sausage?"

"Yes, Filipino pork sausage. Longanisa comes from the Spanish word *longaniza*, which is a spicy, cold pork sausage."

"Lang-o-neezah on my peezza!" said the Kano.

"I'd stick with pepperoni on mine; but here, have some with rice," said the Teacher as he spooned a couple of steaming white mounds from the rice cooker.

"There seems to be a lot going on with rice," said the Kano.

"They say you're not a Filipino unless you have rice with every meal. If the only food in the house is rice, then eat your rice with rice!"

"This breakfast is really good, absolutely delicious."

"*Masarap*," said the Teacher.

"Mah-sah what? Did you say 'Mah-sah-arati'?" asked the Kano. "Why are you talking sports cars when we're eating Filipinos for breakfast, er, eating Filipino?"

"Hah! Masarap is Filipino for 'delicious.' Remember that word, and use it sincerely. It will go a long way, believe me," said the Teacher.

Swallowing, the Kano said, "Mmm, so good. This is definitely comfort food."

"Yes, comfort food is good," said the Teacher. "But Comerford food is even better!"

"Huh? Comer for food? Do you mean come here for food? But I am here," said the Kano.

"Just a little play on words to introduce something I think you'll find interesting. Kano, did you know that the White House Executive Chef is a Filipina?" asked the Teacher.

"Really?"

"Yes, her name is Cristeta Pasia Comerford, she's a Filipino-American, and she's been the Executive Chef since 2005."

"Sounds like she took her cooking skills and love of food to a whole new level."

"She started at the White House in 1995 as an assistant chef; and now, as the Executive Chef, she's the first woman, and the first Asian, to hold the position. She is trained in French classical techniques and specializes in ethnic and American cuisine."

"That's one fringe benefit of the presidency that even I can sink my teeth into."

"Hah! Me too, Kano."

As the Kano started to slow down on his food intake, he said, "Teacher, I think I'm hitting the wall. I've had a few bowls of sinangag, a plate full of tocino—with rice, a bowl of rice, eggs and Spam, corned beef hash and onions—with rice, mini hot dogs—er, I mean Vienna sausages—with rice, some lang-o-neeza—with rice, and a few heavenly pandesal buns—without rice!"

"You've done well. There are some other foods you might see at breakfast—sunny-side-up eggs, sardines in tomato sauce, pork and beans, *puto*, and *tuyo*, which is smoked, dried fish," said the Teacher.

"I can't say I'm disappointed that you didn't have time to make the sardine thing and dried fish," said the Kano. "What's puto?"

"It's a steamed rice cake, a bit heavy, but masarap," said the Teacher.

"Does the dried fish still have its head on?" asked the Kano.

"Yes, and there is a distinct smell to it," said the Teacher.

"A distinct smell? Hmm. Sounds like when a blind date is described as having a nice personality; focusing on the positives?"

"Something like that," laughed the Teacher.

"What are those yellow fruits?"

"Mangoes," said the Teacher. "Here, try one."

With spoon in hand, he scooped out some of the contents of a mango already split in half. It was sliced in sections like a tic-tac-toe board.

"Wow, that's really good. I love the texture," said the Kano.

"Mangoes are among my favorite fruits. Over time, you might be able to identify the various types of Philippine mangoes."

"There's more than one?" mumbled the Kano, his mouth full of the sweet treat.

"Yes, and for some background, the mango originated in India and has become the national fruit of the Philippines. It can be a dessert, a snack, an appetizer, or even part of a main dish. And guess what? According to the Guinness Book of World Records, the biggest mango in the world came from the Philippines and weighed well over seven pounds."

"Bring it on, I can handle it!"

"There's the Carabao mango, Guimaras' Super Galila, Zambales' Sweet Elena, and Guimaras' Talaban and Fresco; also the Indian mango, Apple mango, Horse mango, Pajo or Pahutan mango, and the Evergreen mango, to name a few!"

"Like I've always said, the more mangoes the merrier."

"There are some very beautiful and colorful mango festivals in the Philippines—the Manggahan Festival of Guimaras is celebrated in May and the Mango Festival of Zambales is in April," said the Teacher. "And some Filipinos like to have their mangoes with caviar."

"Caviar? That makes me think of Russian oligarchs. Do Filipino oligarchs like caviar too?"

"Hah! I don't know about oligarchs, but you might hear a Filipino describe the spread they pair their mango with as caviar, but actually it's a shrimp paste called *bagoong*."

"How does the caviar industry feel about being associated with a bag of ohngs?" And what's an ohng, anyway?" The Kano finished off the last square of mango. "Teacher, I still don't understand: How can you just appear out of nowhere?"

"It is strange," admitted the Teacher. "I don't seem to have any control over it, but do know that I am activated by thought waves. Thoughts are vibrations, similar to radio waves, and I can pick up on them—in this case, the vibrations you send out. Although I, like you, am a kano, I love and truly appreciate the Filipino culture; thus, my Filipino spirit is released when someone like yourself is in need of assistance. At the same time, I can maintain my normal self as a father, husband, employee, etc.," said the Teacher.

"Well, I guess I'm glad you're here, even though it's still pitch black outside. Do I have to get up this early every day to get my Filipino on?"

"Like reaching any goal, it all depends on your level of motivation and progress," said the Teacher. "You say that you want to get Maria back, but realistically, you never had her to begin with. That means you're already behind the starting line." He poured the Kano a cup of freshly brewed black coffee.

"Teacher, you are truly wise and I should heed the advice of your counsel, because how did you know I take my coffee black? Is that a Filipino-spirit thingy?"

"No, it's a you're-out-of-milk-or-cream thingy."

"Well, if we are going to be a team, can you tell me how, as a non-Filipino, you came to know and love the culture so much?" asked the Kano.

"Of course. I was a few years younger than you, and much better looking, but my first taste of the Filipino culture was as a US Marine, stationed in southern California. I made some friends, was introduced to the food, and even ate some *balut*."

"Baloot?" asked the young man. "What's that?"

"Let's just say it's a good source of protein. More on that later; I don't want to lose you before we even get started."

"Go on, tell me more."

"My final duty station was Okinawa, Japan. I loved it there, and was able to travel to some other Asian countries, including the Philippines. After my discharge, in a conversation with my father, I remarked that I would probably marry an Asian woman."

"What did he say?"

"Hopefully, she'll be from the Philippines," is what my father said. "Of course, I asked him why."

"Because she'll probably be Catholic," he said.

"Are most Filipinos Catholic?" asked the Kano.

"Yes, about 86 percent of the population is Catholic."

"Hmm," said the Kano. "I guess I never thought of that. I just assumed everybody in that part of the world is Buddhist."

"The Philippines is special for many reasons, one of them being the only Catholic country in that part of the world," said the Teacher. "Most credit Ferdinand Magellan, the Portuguese explorer, with the first attempt to evangelize the country in 1521."

"I guess he was successful."

"I suppose that's right—based on the Philippines' strong Catholic identity today," said the Teacher. "Magellan introduced Christianity, but it did not become established until the 17th century when Spain made the Philippines one of their colonies."

"The rain in Spain falls mainly on the plain."

"Focus, Kano!" said the Teacher. "Anyway, I met my *asawa*, which is Tagalog for 'spouse,' and—"

Interrupting, the Kano asked, "Tag-a-log; is that their language? Sounds like the name of my favorite Girl Scout cookie. Oh, Tag-a-logs are so good—crispy cookies layered with peanut butter and covered with a chocolatey coating. Mmm."

"Kano, those are Tagalongs! Tagalongs! Tagalog is the main dialect of the Philippines, but other languages are spoken too, about 150 in all. Most are classified as Malayo-Polynesian languages," said the Teacher.

"Malayo-Polynesian... sounds exotic," said the Kano.

"They sure do sound exotic—Cebuano, Bikol, and Sambal, to name a few," said the Teacher. "Happily, to make things less complicated, Filipino, or Tagalog, and English, are the official languages of the country. And, the 1987 Philippine Constitution declared Filipino as the national language of the country."

"I wonder what language Maria speaks," said the Kano. "I mean, besides English, which she speaks great."

"She's most likely a Tagalog, and speaks a local dialect as well. And like many Filipino-Americans, she's probably guilty of speaking Taglish," said the Teacher.

"Like Spanglish? asked the Kano. "I saw the movie."

"Yes, something like that."

The Teacher continued. "After being discharged, I returned to college. As I walked into the lecture hall with a hundred or so people already seated, I immediately spotted the beautiful Filipina in the room. She was striking. Just striking."

"And...?"

"Fortunately, I had picked up some Tagalog along the way, and when class was over and she was walking out, I spoke three words that would forever change my life... and hers," said the Teacher.

"What were they?"

"*Pilipina ka ba?*" I asked her, in Tagalog, "Are you Filipina?" I've often thought about that: Three words that entirely changed my life... just happened to be Tagalog."

"Did she answer you back in Filipino?"

"I'm not sure if she did exactly, but she did ask if I spoke Tagalog. Filipinos are like that. If a kano utters even a word or two in Tagalog, they ask if you speak the language. It's wonderful."

"Tell me more."

"To make a long story short," continued the Teacher, "we dated, got engaged, and now we're married for over 28 years, and blessed with four Fil-Ams—our mixed-race, Filipino and American children. But I can remember the first time I met my asawa's family—like your experience, it seemed as if every Filipino within a 100-mile radius was invited! And I'll never forget the smiles. Everyone greeted me with a warm, friendly smile."

"Yes, lots of people. And I forgot to mention," said the Kano, "I got a little thrown when I was introduced to some of Maria's relatives. There was an Uncle Girlie, who was a man, and an Auntie Baby, who was about 60!"

"You'll come to love their naming conventions—they're priceless. And you'll soon find out that *tito* is Filipino for 'uncle' and *tita* means 'aunt.' On my wife's side, I'm a tito— and proud of it! Now, to finish up answering your question, I loved the Filipino culture from my first taste of barbeque and pandesal, and even more so when I married into it. And for reasons I can't explain, I—or more accurately, my Filipino spirit—is occasionally called upon when a kano, such as yourself, cries out for help."

"And the rest of you, as we speak right now—are you saying that you're going about your business as normal, back home?" he asked. "This is really weird."

"You're right, it is weird." The Teacher cleared the table and then turned to a flip chart he had placed in the corner of the kitchen. With a black marker he wrote:

Mannerisms
Geography
History

"Looking at this flip chart makes me feel like I'm back in school," said the Kano.

"If you want to be a student of the Filipino culture and try to win Maria's heart, then, yes, you are back in school.

Are you going to be an *A* student? I only have room in my class for *A* students," said the Teacher.

"But I'm the only student in your class."

"Kano!"

"Yes, yes, I'll be an *A* student," he said grudgingly. "Can I ask you a question?"

"Yes. Is that it?"

"Is that what?" asked the Kano.

"The question."

"I haven't asked it yet."

"Hmm, it sounded like a question. Oh well, what is it?"

"I get geography. And I get history. But mannerisms? As subjects of study? Maybe I'll just come back when you start on geography, and get a few more winks of my beauty sleep."

"It's not like you couldn't use some. Have you looked in the mirror this morning? Getting up before sunrise doesn't suit you well."

"Uh, I don't think I'd be getting up so early if you-know-who didn't appear in you-know-who's room at you-know-what time."

"Where's you appreciation, Kano? I mean your—*your* appreciation, Kano. If I wasn't here to train you, I could still be in bed!"

"But you are still in bed!" said the Kano. "Remember, right now, you are only your Filipino spirit, and the rest of you is snuggled up in bed, sleeping!"

"Oh, that's right. And I'm quite comfy. We just got some new linens and a couple of those MyPillows. Now, no more talk of sleep; let's continue with your instruction," said the Teacher.

"So by mannerisms, I guess you mean things like how Filipinos talk with their eyebrows?"

"Yes, that's right. Tell me again what you observed at Maria's party," said the Teacher.

"I noticed a lot of eyebrows going up and down. Sometimes, it happened when people greeted each other; other times, to sort of acknowledge things said in a conversation; or, other times, a sort of 'Hmm, what's wrong with you?' look, like when I made my karaoke remark."

"Yes, the raising of the eyebrows, and forehead for that matter, is a mannerism I don't think you'll find among anyone else. It almost seems to be genetic, something in their DNA," said the Teacher.

"Raising of eyebrows—also known as eyebrow talk— is a sign of non-verbal communication—check," said the Kano, making a check in the air with his index finger.

The Teacher continued. "The next mannerism I'd like to talk about has to do with lips. Why do you think we need to discuss this?"

"Well, I think you mean the lip pointing, or the pointing of lips. At first, I almost mistook it for something else!" said the Kano. "If you know what I mean."

"I'm glad you came to your senses quickly. But I understand. At first it seems, well, a little different. But, for Filipinos who have grown up in the Philippines or were raised by Filipino parents while living abroad, pointing with lips becomes second nature."

"It seems to be somewhat directional," said the Kano.

"It makes sense, if you think about it. Just imagine having your hands full of grocery bags, or boxes, or even a baby, and your arms are tied up. And someone asks you for directions. Can you see how easy it is to point them in the right direction? Just purse your lips, combine with an eyebrow/head raise action, and lip point in the appropriate direction. No need to even talk!"

"I see your point. Sounds like 'hands-free' was invented by the Filipino!" said the Kano.

"You know, my wife doesn't eyebrow talk or lip point as much as she used to," said the Teacher, a little sad.

"No?"

"My asawa came to this country when she was 17, so she grew up in a full, 360-degree surround-sound Filipino home and culture. In our old VHS home video recordings, she is eyebrow talking and lip pointing quite frequently, far more than she does now. Heck, even I was doing it quite a bit back then!"

"And you miss those mannerisms?" asked the Kano.

"Yes, yes, I guess I do. Not that she doesn't do it at all. But we've been married for over 28 years, living in a household that is more kano than *Pinoy,* so some of those mannerisms and habits are not as prominent as they used to be."

Filipinos invented hands-free

"Do I see a tear? I'm serious, Teacher. Are you sad? Even just a little?"

"Enough about me, Kano," said the Teacher, clearing his throat. "And enough about mannerisms, since I think we've covered the most obvious two—lip pointing and eyebrow talk. Though, I suppose I should mention nose talk, although that isn't exactly a mannerism."

"Nose talk? What do you mean?" asked the Kano.

"Well, yes, I've never really understood it—not that all Filipinos make comments on their noses—and I think it's more of a female than male thing; but let's say some wish their noses were less flat. *Pangos* and *tangos*, that about sums it up."

"Pangos, tangos and mangoes, oh my," said the Kano. Clearing his throat nervously, he said, "Uh, what do you mean by pangos and tangos?"

"Pango means 'flat.' My wife, for example, thinks her nose is flat, but I think it adorns her beautiful face like a crown jewel."

"Oh, how sweet."

"And tango means 'pointed.' I suppose some Filipinas think a more pointed nose is desirable, but I completely disagree! It's perfect the way it is. Now, as we begin your training, here's a great observation to remember that's been made of Filipinos—that they are Malay in family, Spanish in love, Chinese in business, and American in ambition. And, it's an observation rooted in respect and affection."

"I'm not exactly sure what that means, Teacher, but I'm anxious to find out. Anything that will help me win Maria's heart."

"Okay, let's start with some basics. Tell me what you know about the geography of the Philippines."

"Not much, I guess," answered the Kano. "It's somewhere by China, isn't it?"

"Yes, in a way, but about 2,000 miles south. It's an archipelago of over 7,000 islands, and—"

"Seven thousand islands? Wow, that's a lot!" said the Kano.

"There's a lot of them, that's for sure," said the Teacher. "And the islands are divided into three groups—Luzon, Visayas, and Mindanao."

"All right, got it. Seven thousand islands, south of China, three main groups—check," said the Kano, using his right index finger to make another check in the air. "What else?"

"There are a number of volcanos. Probably the most famous is Mt. Pinatubo. It's known as the most destructive volcano in the world."

"Really; why?"

"In 1991, it erupted and not only caused damage to the Philippines but spread its ashes all over the world, causing all kinds of damage," said the Teacher.

"Maybe that can work for me," said the Kano.

"Huh?"

"It can be the inspiration for a poem I'll write for Maria. That my love is so strong, not even an active volcano like Pinatubo can keep me away from her."

"Sheesh, you're sounding kind of *OA*," said the Teacher.

"OA?"

"Over acting," said the Teacher.

"Huh? I've never heard that before."

"I think you're going to hear a lot of it," the Teacher chuckled.

"Okay, so lots of islands and volcanos—check," said the Kano. "Can you tell me more?"

"I like your eagerness, Kano, and we're just getting started." The Teacher consulted the flip chart. "History," he said. "What do you know about the history of the Philippines?"

"Hmm. Not much. Really, nothing, other than watching that old John Wayne movie, *Back to Bataan*."

"That was a classic, but there's much more to the Philippines than World War II. Do you know why the country is called the Philippines?"

"Some guy named Phil discovered it?" joked the Kano.

"In a way, and no ordinary Phil. It was named in honor of the King of Spain, Phillip II. That's where the name of the Philippines comes from."

"Way to go, Phil!"

"So you'll see a lot of Spanish influence," said the Teacher. "From surnames to names of cities to customs and holidays. That can happen during 333 years of Spanish rule—and, it's why Catholicism became so fixed—through the work of Catholic missionaries over the centuries. The faith has permanently influenced the culture and society of the Philippines—and for me, it's a reason why the Filipino people are so special."

"What can you tell me about their more recent history?" asked the Kano.

"There are a few things you should know about, but let me say one more thing about the Spanish influence on the Philippines," said the Teacher.

35

"Go on."

"The Filipinos are a proud people—rightly so. They didn't simply lie down and accept everything the Spaniards transported over," said the Teacher. "They used their own values and principles to balance the new cultural influences and retain their old—and accepted only those that fitted their nature and character.

"But, regarding recent history, let me give you a few key names and events that will help you know more about this fascinating country," said the Teacher.

"Great."

"I may test you, so please pay attention."

"Yes, sir!"

"Dr. Jose Rizal, considered one of the greatest heroes of the Philippines, fought the Spanish government and was executed in 1896 for rebellion," said the Teacher.

"Jose Rizal, check," said the Kano.

"Wait, I'm not done. He was a Filipino nationalist, and an ophthalmologist by profession. It was his advocacy for reforms in the Philippines that led to his execution by the Spanish colonial government. He was charged with the crime of rebellion, in part because of his writings. He was young, only 36. But his death ignited his country's opposition against the Spanish government. They say Rizal inspired the nation to be born."

"Rizal, Jose. Check and check," said the Kano, making two air checks this time. "What a legacy."

"The year 1898 is pretty significant."

"My great grandmother was born in 1898," said the Kano. "In Paterson, New Jersey. Why is that year significant for Filipinos?"

"June 12 is Independence Day in the Philippines—it's a national holiday and commemorates the Philippine Declaration of Independence from Spain on June 12, 1898. A few months later, on December 10, 1898, the Treaty of Paris was signed between the United States and Spain. This ended the Spanish-American War and gave the Philippines to America for a payment of $20 million."

"Hmm, that's kind of strange. Sounds like the Philippines sort of passed from one country to another."

"Well, not exactly, and it is complicated, worthy of further study on your part. But fortunately, on July 4, 1946, the Treaty of Manila was signed. This is when the US recognized Philippine independence and ended the Commonwealth. It's thought of as the Philippine Independence from America."

"July 4, just like us," said the Kano.

"You should also know about Manuel Quezon. He became President in 1935 and was the first Filipino to head a government of the entire Philippines. Under his leadership, the country adopted Tagalog as the national language."

"Quezon, President, check."

"December 8, 1941, began the Japanese invasion of the Philippines. It was horrible," said the Teacher.

"Yes, I saw some of that in the *Back to Bataan* movie I mentioned."

"Luckily, in 1944, US General Douglas MacArthur made his famous return, which began the retaking of the Philippines from the Japanese," said the Teacher.

"'I shall return,'" said the Kano. "I think I remember that from my high school history class."

"As an aside, if you want to catch Maria's attention, when you excuse yourself to go to another room temporarily, say '*Babilik ako*,' which means 'I shall return.'"

"Bah... .bah... leek... ahh... ko," said the Kano, very slowly and deliberately.

"That's right, but don't take as long to say it as the great General's return was to the Philippines," said the Teacher.

"No problem."

Another important event for you to know is September 21, 1972, when President Ferdinand Marcos declared martial law. This ushered in a difficult time. He abolished the Congress, took over many businesses, and imprisoned people critical of the government."

"Sounds scary. How long did it last?" asked the Kano.

"About 14 years," said the Teacher. "Marcos was eventually exiled to Hawaii."

"Why?"

"Probably for lots of reasons, but two significant events that lit the flames of change were the assassination of Senator Benigno Aquino in 1983 and the election of his widow, Corazon Aquino, in 1986," said the Teacher.

"Wait, Aquino? I thought I heard some of the men talking politics at Maria's house. Was the previous president of the Philippines named Aquino?" asked the Kano.

"Yes, Benigno Aquino III. He is the son of Senator Benigno and Corazon."

"Uh-huh. And it was remarkable how the senator's widow came to power," said the Teacher. "It was known as The People Power Revolution… some refer to it as the Yellow Revolution."

"Why is that?"

"When Senator Aquino was assassinated, the people demonstrated in protest, along with lots of yellow ribbons," said the Teacher. "They demanded Cory, his wife, be placed as president, which happened on February 25, 1986. She restored democracy to the country."

"Wow, amazing. I'm really interested in knowing more about the history of the Philippines."

"Good Kano, that's good. We can only cover a few important points right now. I'm glad you want to learn more. Now, something I wasn't planning on discussing today—it doesn't exactly fit under geography and history, but I'm afraid we'll be so busy the next few days that I'll forget… maybe, I think I'll…." the Teacher trailed off as he turned back toward the flip chart and wrote the word *erythromycin* on it.

"Eee rye thro… Teacher, that's a lot of letters—is it one of those really long Tagaly words?"

"No, it's English. Erythromycin. It's an antibiotic," said the Teacher. "And it's Tagalog, not Tagaly. Or Tagalong!"

"Uh, sorry. It's just that I'm… a little hungry still," said the Kano. "Is Filipino food like Chinese food? You know, you're hungry again 15 minutes after eating it?"

"I never believed that myth, but when it comes to Filipino food, if you come back to the table in 15 minutes to eat again, it's because the food is so good! Now, where were we? Oh, yes. I don't think it's an exaggeration to say that the discovery of erythromycin is one of the most significant medical breakthroughs in history. The drug was an alternative antibiotic for penicillin-allergic patients."

"Uh-huh. Yes, go on."

"Remember the name Dr. Abelardo B. Aguilar, because sadly, it's a name not very well known," said the Teacher, "and it should be."

"Why? And, who is he?" asked the Kano.

"Dr. Aguilar was a Filipino, working in the western Visayas of the Philippines as a physician and medical representative for Eli Lilly."

"Lilly? The drug company? My cousin is a sales rep for them," said the Kano.

"Yes, yes. Well, as the story goes, Dr. Aguilar sent Lilly a soil sample for testing, and this sample eventually became the source for erythromycin, a drug that has saved millions and millions of lives. Interestingly, when the drug launched in 1952, it was under the brand name Ilosone, named after the Philippine region of Iloilo where Aguilar collected it."

"Teacher, I don't understand. If Dr. Aguilar discovered erythromycin, and through doing so, saved countless lives, shouldn't I know who he is? Like how we all know about Louis Pasteur, the father of vaccines?"

"Should know, yes. I agree. But you don't, nor do most people. The short answer is that Lilly simply would not credit him for the discovery, either in recognition or compensation."

"That seems awfully unfair, Teacher," said the Kano. "Why would they do that?"

"I really don't know why. Lilly claimed the discovery was the intellectual property of the company, and their position was that no employee receives royalties or compensation beyond their salary or benefits."

"Still, Dr. Aguilar should be recognized and celebrated!"

"It's really a travesty. Erythromycin treats bacterial infections, pneumonia, ear and skin infections, and the list goes on and on. It's a miracle drug that has saved millions of lives and made Lilly countless billions of dollars," said the Teacher. "And, how many people know that the source of this discovery was the Philippines?"

"Not enough," said the Kano. "Not even close to enough."

"Dr Aguilar tried in vain to seek compensation from Eli Lilly. He wanted to use the money to help the poor and sick in the Philippines, but it never came."

"Teacher, that just wasn't right."

"Yes. But, it didn't stop Aguilar from helping the poor and sick in his own hometown of Iloilo City. He became known as the 'doctor of the poor' because most of his patients were too poor to pay him."

"I feel guilty now," said the Kano.

"Why?"

"Because all I'm thinking about is my stomach, while Dr. Aguilar was thinking about his suffering countrymen."

"Kano, I'm glad to hear you say that, and I don't doubt that you're sincere. But I've seen you eat—and I have a sneaking suspicion that you'll get over it!"

Mysteriously and without warning, the Teacher and the Kano found themselves standing on a deserted beach, the sounds of the waves washing ashore.

"Teacher, what happened? We were just in the kitchen, and now we are... we're... well, I'm not exactly sure where we are."

"To be honest, Kano, neither am I. But standing on a deserted beach with the sound of the ocean behind us is the perfect backdrop we need to assess your progress, and determine if you can move forward."

"Assess my progress? If I can move forward? Teacher, I thought you wanted to teach me The Way of the Filipino? This sounds like I'm under double-secret probation or something."

"It's no secret, Kano. But you are under a probation of sorts, as you told me you want to win Maria's heart, isn't that right? You seem sincere, since you've triggered and activated my Filipino spirit. That's not something you can fake. But, you don't get a trophy just for showing up. To *learn* The Way of the Filipino, you need to *earn* The Way of the Filipino. And you do that by embracing the knowledge I'm sharing with you, and... and..."

"And what, Teacher?"

"Something more. There needs to be something more... something more than just the acquisition of knowledge."

"Something more? Like eating some more of those lumpy shanghai things?"

"Kano, lumpia! Lumpia shanghai! That's not the 'something more' I'm alluding to, but for your training, they do serve to symbolize the successful progression of your transformation."

"Yes, my transformation. Will it be like the *Transformers* movie? I always dreamed of being an autobot."

"Kano! This is serious. Don't you want to win Maria's heart? Your transformation means to step out of your kano-ness so that you may fully embrace the Filipino culture—and genuinely appreciate all it has to offer."

"Embrace, culture, appreciate," mumbled the Kano, talking out loud to himself as he wrote the words on a small notepad. Looking up, he asked, "And the 'something more' part? What's that again?" I'll write it down too."

"How did you get a notepad and pen on this deserted beach? Oh well, never mind. Listen, Kano, these things you're learning about—you don't simply write them down and check them off. What you're doing—or should be doing, is more than just learning. It's becoming. And the 'something more'? I'll know it when I see it. More importantly, you'll know it."

"Maybe you'll know it, but me? How will I know? I'm just a kano."

"Believe me, you'll know."

"Okay, well, all this training today has made me hungry. You do have a lumpy... er, a lumpia shanghai, don't you?" asked the Kano against the sounds of the ocean waves breaking upon shoreline.

"I sure do," said the Teacher as he put out his closed, right hand, palm up, and slowly uncurled his fingers to reveal the light brown lumpia shanghai he was holding. "But tell me why I should give this to you."

"Because I learned many things today, Teacher, and appreciated them! Starting off with a delicious Filipino breakfast with foods like tocino, longanisa, and pandesal, and discovering that the White House Chef is a Filipina, Chef Comerford. I learned about the geography of the Philippines and its 7,000 islands, and the Spanish and Catholic influence that has shaped the country."

"Yes, very good Kano. Anything else?"

"Inspiring historical giants like Jose Rizal, Manuel Quezon, and Cory Aquino—heroes of the Philippines, for sure. I'm going to read more about them—and, the country's history. My education has just begun!" said the Kano enthusiastically.

The Teacher smiled. He was pleased. Placing the lumpia shanghai in the Kano's hand, he said, "You have passed for now. There is more to come."

Biting into the crisp lumpia, the Kano said, "That's good, Teacher—I'm going to need a lot more than one to fill me up. Uh, can these lumpy things be supersized?"

"Uy!"

CHAPTER 3
DUCK FOR COVER

The Kano tossed and turned in his sleep. He mumbled incoherently, kicked at the covers, and fussed with the pillows. Then he awoke abruptly and sat up in bed, breathing heavily.

"You're having a nightmare, aren't you, Kano?" came a voice from the darkness.

"Teacher, is that you? I didn't hear the alarm. Is it 5 a.m. yet?" The eye-squinting Kano asked sleepily. "I think I hear my stomach growling, maybe that's what woke me up."

"No, it's not 5 a.m. It's still the middle of the night. You didn't hear the alarm because it hasn't gone off yet. And yes, that is your stomach growling. How can you sleep through all that gurgling? Are you never not hungry?"

"They say the key to proper nutrition is to eat small meals throughout the day. I'm just following the advice of the experts."

"You contacted Maria yesterday?" asked the Teacher, sounding as inquisitive as he was stern.

"Uh, how did you know?" asked the Kano nervously. He sensed the Teacher was about to reprimand him.

"I have ways. You are feeling guilty and foolish over your behavior with Maria yesterday, isn't that right? As you drifted off to sleep, that guilt caused you to have a nightmare, which has resulted in a tremendous amount of your thought vibrations being released into the ether, which my Filipino spirit picked up on. Because you are now my student, these thought vibrations immediately summoned me to you."

"You say you have ways? What does that mean? And, I'm allowed to dream, aren't I? Was that part of this deal? It's not like I'm in some kind of Filipino boot camp or something; right, Teacher? No freedom of personal movement? Or thought? I mean, am I allowed to try to win Maria over on my own, even before you let me Manny Pak-e-ow you?"

"Mano-po, Kano. Not Manny Pak-e-ow. It's Mano-po. No, you're not in boot camp. And yes, you can try to win back Maria. But…"

"But what?"

"But right now, you're not ready. And don't forget, you agreed to this instruction and training. Without it, you'll make things worse, like you did yesterday, apparently. You must be patient, you must train properly. You'll know you're making progress with each lumpia shanghai that I give you. At some point, when I think you've been Filipino'd enough, you'll be ready to go out on your own."

"Oh yeah? Well, if you're telling me that you have a crystal ball or something, then I guess you know that I had a date with Maria yesterday for coffee, to try to patch things up. If I say so myself, I thought it went rather well."

"Date? Went well? Then why the nightmare?"

"Well, uh, not exactly a *date* date, but a meeting date—yes, a meeting of two mature people, with uh, food, and conversation and—"

"Kano, you don't sound convinced that this was any kind of a date, nor that it went well."

"Well, maybe it wasn't a perfect date, as far as dates go, but I think I made some progress with Maria. I mean, she agreed to meet, we talked, we laughed, we—"

"Kano!" interrupted the Teacher. "Unless you're honest with yourself, you'll never be honest with Maria. And, you'll never win her back. Now tell me what really happened."

Sigh. "Teacher, I was incredibly insensitive, in fact, sort of mean, when at the coffee shop she pulled out a, I, uh, it really wasn't a snack; she said it was a snack, but it was a..."

"A what, Kano?"

"A duck!"

"I'm confused. Are you saying she brought a pet duck with her to the coffee shop?" asked the Teacher.

"No, her duck wasn't a pet. It was a snack!"

"Well, that's not so odd. I mean, have you ever had Peking Duck? It's delicious. She probably just brought a *baon* with her from last night's dinner."

"Bayonne? Did you say 'Bayonne,' as in Bayonne, NJ? No, we were a couple of towns over—"

"Not Bayonne, baon. Bah-own. You can think of baon as sort of a doggy bag—not exactly the same, but that's the idea."

"Teacher, anyway, getting back to yesterday and Maria. You must know of this... this... this food."

"Kano, yes, of course I know. It sounds like Maria brought along a nice snack of balut."

"Uh, yes, baloot... baloot. That's what she called it."

"She called it balut-balut?"

"No, baloot. She called it baloot."

When you know you've waited too long to eat the balut

"And when you saw it, you probably were stand-offish and rude. Is that what happened?"

"Sort of."

"Kano, did you ever play a sport in high school?"

"Huh? Well, yes, football. But what has that got to do with—"

"And on Mondays, did your coach review videos of Saturday's game, so that the players could observe themselves, as they actually played?"

"Yes."

"And the purpose was to observe what the team did right and did wrong and to figure out how to improve; wouldn't you agree?"

"Yes, that's right, Teacher."

"Well, we're going to do the same."

"Huh? The same? How? Nobody was filming my date… er, my meeting with Maria yesterday."

"Earlier, you joked about me having a crystal ball, remember?"

"Yes. Do you?"

"It's not exactly a ball. But here, look at this!" said the Teacher as he pulled something out from behind his back.

"Aah!" shrieked the Kano while pulling the bedcovers up close to his chin. "That's it, that's the egg thingy Maria had yesterday."

"Yes, this is my special balut," said the Teacher, clearing his throat. "Balut egg."

"Baloot-baloot egg?"

"No, just balut, Kano."

"And why is your baloot-baloot... er, I mean baloot egg, so special, Teacher?"

"Because it's not an ordinary balut egg. This egg is more like a crystal ball."

"A crystal ball-loot?"

"Hey, ball-loot. That's pretty good, Kano. Yes, I only have to rub the shell of this balut egg, and tune the vibrations of my thoughts to the Kano I'm trying to help, like you, and—"

"And what, then you can see me? But this happened yesterday. What did you do, send a baloot drone into the coffee shop to spy on us and take video? I don't remember seeing any flying eggs," laughed the Kano, seeming confident the Teacher didn't have anything on him.

"Kano, like me, my special crystal-ball balut isn't bound by space or time."

"And that means...?"

"Just think of this balut egg as having instant replay."

"Oh no, I'm cooked."

"No Kano. Like the balut, you are not cooked. At least not fully. You can still redeem yourself. But to win back Maria, you've got to stop being so culturally insensitive, and just plain obnoxious."

"Sorry, Teacher."

"Don't tell me you're sorry. Tell Maria. But tell her in your actions and behaviors, not in empty words."

"Okay, what should I do?"

"We must first expose you to the light of truth. Look into this balut egg, and just like watching a game film, you can see how you acted yesterday."

"Okay, I'm ready for my close-up, Teacher."

With that, the Teacher closed his eyes and rubbed the balut egg. The shell's color slowly went from white to opaque, to displaying yesterday's scene in the coffee shop. He opened his eyes, and both he and the Kano stared into the egg, and watched the previous day's events unfold.

"Uh, hi, Maria," said the Kano nervously as he stood up from the table he was sitting at to greet her.

"Hi."

"Here's your hot ginger tea."

"Thanks for ordering it for me," she said, somewhat reserved.

"I'm really sorry about the party, you know, for being a bit awkward."

"I don't think you were awkward."

"Really," said the Kano, feeling a bit encouraged.

"I thought you were rude."

"Oh."

"Inviting you to a big family party, after just meeting you, was kind of a big deal for me," she said.

"Me too. I was really honored."

"Then why did you act so, so, not nice?"

"Well, I wouldn't say I wasn't nice, I was just—"

"Just what? Just being you? Are you saying that you're naturally rude?"

"Maria, do you think I was rude? I mean, there were a lot of people, and different languages, and strange—I mean different—kinds of foods, and…"

"Yes, some of my relatives and guests were speaking Tagalog, and probably another dialect or two. And those foods are foods of my culture. I thought you'd be interested in that part of me. You certainly seemed to give me that impression when we first met."

"Uh, yes, of course. But it was, well, it was all new to me. I felt really bad afterwards. That's why I invited you for a cup of coffee, to apologize."

"Really? You want to apologize?"

"Yes, please forgive me. I'm open to new things, believe me, but sometimes I'm a little slow to warm up."

"Well, I guess I can see that, but you were the first, you know, someone that wasn't Filipino, who I invited to a family party."

"Well, I can assure you Maria, that's all behind me now. I'm going to learn about all things Filipino, and be open, and sensitive, and appreciative and… *Aah!* What's that?"

Maria had taken something out a bag she'd brought along that looked like the half of a large, cracked egg and placed it on the table in front of her. "What's this, you ask? It's my snack. I like it with tea."

Trembling, the Kano asked, "S… s… snack?"

"Yes. Would you like some?" she asked, offering the Kano the embryonic egg as it sat in the palm of her hand.

"*Aah!*" screamed the Kano. "It's a half-birthed baby chicken!"

"It's balut! What's wrong with you?"

"What's wrong with me? Me? Nothing is wrong with me. I eat my chicken fried, or grilled, or McNugget-ed, not raw! *Ewww!*" he shrieked.

"It's not chicken, it's duck." Maria then drank the broth from the inside, peeled off the shell and bit into the balut.

"*Aah!*" screamed the Kano as he leapt up from the table, jumped from foot to foot as if he were on hot coals, and shook his hands as if his fingertips were on fire. "*Eww, eww!*"

"Michael, you're making a scene. And embarrassing me. Please, stop it. Sit down. People are looking. Please!"

Catching his breath, he said, "*Ahh*, oh, sorry, sorry."

"Sorry? Again? Yes, you sure look sorry, Michael."

"Maria, please, give me a chance. Tell me more about this chicken, er, duck. This duck dish."

Maria sighs. "Okay, like I said, it's called balut and it's very good, a not uncommon food in the Philippines. Street food, you could say."

"Okay."

"It's a fertilized bird egg, typically a duck. Usually goes through two to three weeks of incubation, then you boil or steam it, and eat it right out of the shell. The bones are soft enough to chew and swallow."

Gulp. "Yes, mmm, okay. I think I can… I think I, um, understand," said the Kano.

"Some people add a little salt or vinegar to it, and it's not only eaten in the Philippines but in Laos, Cambodia, Thailand, and Vietnam."

"Good, that's good," said the Kano, still not having fully recovered from watching Maria slurp and eat the balut only moments ago.

"In Tagalog and Malay, the word *balut* means 'wrapped.'"

"Wrapped?"

"I guess it has something to do with the shell. Anyway, balut is a good source of nutrition. Each egg has about 14 grams of protein, 188 calories, and around 100 milligrams of calcium," said Maria. "I love the yolk, *mmm*, it's so good. The texture is soft and dissolves in your mouth, almost like a mousse."

"Like a mouse? A mouse? Did you say 'mouse'? I, I, I—"

"Mousse! Not mouse! Mousse! You know, like the dessert. What's wrong with you, Michael? You're so quick to judge."

"Uh, I'm… uh, really, now that you've described it, it does sound pretty, pretty tasty. *Mmm*, yes, it does. I'll try some at the next party, for sure—that is, if you invite me."

"You won't have to worry about that, Michael."

"I, uh, I understand, Maria," said the Kano, disappointed, assuming she was breaking things off before they even began. "I had my chance."

"I mean that you don't have to wait until another party to try balut. Here, I brought another one," said Maria happily as she pulled another egg out of her bag.

"Oh, yes, yes, that looks really good, but, I did, I mean, I did have an extra-large coffee before you came and a donut, and I, I'm not really hungry right now, and—"

"You're not going to try it?" asked Maria.

"Really, next party, I'm saving my appetite. First thing I'll put on my plate, no doubt."

"Hmm, okay," said Maria skeptically as she slowly cracked open the balut egg, drank the broth and downed the contents in two bites, chewing slowly as the Kano watched her, transfixed on the feather she deliberately let dangle from her lower lip. "You can eat balut next time. But right now, you can kiss me."

"Kiss you? Right now? Here? In full public view?" he said, still transfixed on the feather that Maria purposely let hang from her lower lip. "I'm, I'm shy, you know? Well, I've really got to go," said the Kano as he got up clumsily from the table. "You just had some baloot, and I'm sure you're busy, and maybe you want to gargle and…"

"Michael, I knew your extra-large coffee and donut excuse was just that—an excuse!"

"Okay, you're right, you're right," said the Kano, as he stopped himself from leaving. "I'm ready. Do you have another one? I'm really ready—seriously, I'm ready to eat some baloot. I really think I'm, uh, ready, really, for sure."

"Goodbye, Michael!"

With that, the crystal ball balut egg's shell transformed back to its normal off-white color. The Kano looked up to face the Teacher's stare.

"Kano, that was a disaster," said the Teacher.

"I know, I know. You don't have to tell me. Did you hear how she said goodbye? Emphasis on the 'bye' part of that word. That hurt."

"Hurt? Kano, it was you who hurt Maria. This is her culture, and you're so, unappreciative of how really incredible it is. I don't doubt you care for her, but why are you so... so you?"

Sighing. "I don't know, but I do know this, Teacher. Somehow, some way, I'll show Maria I'm all in. All in."

"Then get some rest, Kano. You've got your work cut out for you."

CHAPTER 4
THE FIRST SHALL BE LAST

"Kano, wake up, wake up," said the Teacher as he shook the Kano's shoulder. "Time to get up."

"Huh?"

"It's 4:57 a.m. I guess you couldn't wait three more minutes to see me, as the vibrations of your thoughts have activated me. You were dreaming about me, Kano?" asked the Teacher. "How flattering."

"Uh, dreaming… of you?" asked the Kano, wiping the sleep out of his eyes. "Not a chance. I was dreaming of marrying Maria. Teacher, can't we accelerate this training of yours? Every day that passes is another day someone else may win Maria's heart."

"Kano, it's not my instruction and training, it's yours. So far, I've only given you one lumpia shanghai. There is much more for you to learn. Even then, there's no guarantee. There has to be something more to all of this than just eating lumpia shanghai."

"There's that 'something more' thing again."

"Get yourself ready and come downstairs to the kitchen. We have a really important subject to cover."

"Hmm… I must say, Teacher, you do make strong and great tasting coffee," said the Kano as he sat down at the kitchen table with a cup in hand. "Just what I need when I'm up before the early bird. Worms don't stand a chance when I'm around."

The Teacher was writing on the flip chart, but his back partly obscured the view, so the Kano couldn't see exactly what was written. The Teacher turned around and asked the Kano, "What is written on the bottom?"

"3M?" he answered.

"Huh?"

"3M. It's on the bottom. In the corner."

"No, on the bottom, but not the bottom bottom. 3M is the name of the company that made this flip chart. Look below the other subjects you've learned about—that bottom."

"Well, you did say 'bottom,' Teacher. I think most people would think the bottom of the page is…." The Kano stopped suddenly. The Teacher's face was getting red. "Early Immigration. Yes sir, that's what's on the bottom of the flip chart. You just wrote 'Early Immigration.'"

"Yes, 'Early Immigration.' What does that mean to you?"

"Hmm, not much, really. Should it?"

"Yes, it should. Because if it wasn't for the courageous Filipinos who first immigrated to the United States, it's likely Maria wouldn't be here. Just as likely my wife wouldn't have made it here. And if my wife wasn't a Filipino immigrant to the United States, we wouldn't have married, and had four children. My Fil-Am children would never have been born. Think about that, Kano. The debt of gratitude I have to every—and I mean every—early Filipino immigrant, can never be repaid."

"Teacher, I understand what you're saying—you know, that you had to meet your wife to have children and all, but aren't you, maybe making a bit too much of this early immigration thing?"

Topping off the Kano's cup with some more coffee, the Teacher said, "Not at all. In fact, far too little of it has been made, and it's a story that needs to be told more often, with more voices—non-Filipino voices as much as Filipino ones."

"I see. So what do I need to know about?" asked the Kano.

Taking a deep breath, the Teacher asked out loud, almost to himself, "Where to begin? The Manila-Acapulco galleon trade? The Thomasites? *Pensionados?* The sugar cane and pineapple fields of Hawaii? The Alaskeros and Manila men? World War II? Watsonville, California? Carlos Bulosan?"

"Teacher, I'm sorry. I can't, can't… follow. I don't know what you're talking about."

"My apologies, Kano. There's just so much here. As much as kanos like you who have an interest in Filipino culture should know this history, I suspect there's a whole lot of second-generation Filipinos and Fil-Ams, like my children, who don't know much of it either. Maybe even some first-generation Filipinos too."

"Teacher, you seem so serious—and, a bit, I don't know... sad. Are you feeling sad right now, Teacher?"

"In a way, I guess I am, because what I have to teach you about the early Filipino immigrants to America is difficult. Difficult for me to discuss because it was so difficult for them—and oppressive and far too often unfair. But from that struggle came triumph, for the millions of Filipinos who followed and prospered in this country. That's the great corollary."

"Core-oh-Larry? Teacher, that's a big word for me. Core-oh-Larry? I don't think you're referring to my core, which I must say, is pretty amazing. *Are* you referring to my amazing core?" asked the Kano, as he stared down at his midsection and admiringly tapped his abs with his fingertips.

"No, I'm not referring to your amazing core. I said *corollary*, meaning 'result.' The tremendous difficulties and hardships of the early Filipino settlers to America paved the way for greater assimilation and economic prosperity for those who followed."

"I really would like to learn about this history, Teacher. Do you think Maria is familiar with it?"

"I don't know. You should ask."

"I will. But, what's the most important part of the story that I should know about?" asked the Kano.

"It's all important, starting about 500 years ago with the Spanish galleons."

"Gallons? Spanish gallons? Like in gallons of sangria? I am a bit thirsty, Teacher. And where's breakfast this morning? I don't see any tasty Filipinos for breakfast. Er, food, Filipino food, for breakfast."

"Stop thinking about your amazing stomach! Galleons as in ships, not gallons as in liquid measurement. Spanish trading ships. For 250 years this route linked the Philippines with Mexico across the Pacific Ocean, despite its treacherous navigating conditions."

"Uh, Teacher, I'm no geography scholar, but you're describing something between Mexico and the Philippines, not America and the Philippines."

"Stay with me. The Manila-Acapulco trade route began around 1565 when a galleon set sail from the Philippine city of Cebu for Acapulco, Mexico. These galleons were built in the shipyards of Cavite, outside Manila, by Filipino craftsmen. Other galleons followed, and over the next two centuries, many hundreds, if not thousands, of Filipinos were conscripted as the crew. Filipinos were by nature a great seafaring people, and they brought tremendous knowledge and experience to these voyages."

"Mm-hmm."

"But crewmen were often brutalized and mistreated by the ship's officers, and it wasn't uncommon to jump ship in Acapulco or California to escape. It's believed some Filipinos traveled the shorelines between Mexico and the southern parts of the US, looking for a suitable place to settle."

"Where did they land, so to speak?" asked the Kano.

"We know from written accounts in the 1760s, there was a large numbers of Filipinos who had settled in the bayous of Louisiana, in an area called Saint Malo, and were known as Manilamen and Tagalas. They lived in small houses, which were supported above the water by stilts, and they largely governed themselves separate from the broader community. They made their living off the sea, and actually created the fish and shrimp drying industry, which still exists today!"

"Ahh, so interesting. Now I see the American connection. But is it okay if I don't like dried fish?"

"Kano, you don't have to like every single Filipino food. Not every Filipino loves balut. Now, do you remember yesterday when I told you about the Treaty of Paris?"

"Yes, I remember. I was hoping that it might have something to do with the Eiffel Tower, or french fries. I love french fries."

"Kano! I'm establishing a timeline here. As you learned yesterday, the Treaty of Paris, in 1898, ended the Spanish-American War and gave the Philippines to the US for $20 million."

"I know $20 million is a lot of money, especially back then. But still, for a whole country? I've recently heard of penthouses sold in Manhattan for $50 million!"

"Yes, I don't know. The spoils of war, as they say. But, this did end the Spanish Colonial Period of the Philippines, which lasted from 1521 to 1898."

"But you told me that the Philippines then became a territory of the US. Why couldn't it just be set free?"

"They tried. In August of 1898, General Emilio Aguinaldo declared Philippine independence from Spain and sought international recognition for it, but America simply ignored the general."

"Teacher, even so, when Spain ceded the Philippines to the US, Filipinos were kind of... kind of happy about that, right?" asked the Kano, hopefully.

"Not exactly, at least not everyone. I don't think it's that well known, but after the treaty was signed, there was a revolt against the US known as the Philippine Insurrection, which went on for over three years. Ten times more US troops died suppressing this insurrection than in defeating Spain. It was also called the Philippine-American War."

"The Philippine-American War? Wow, that seems so... so opposite of how I think of our connection, you know? Fighting each other? Because our two countries are, I mean, we're friends; right, Teacher?"

"We are. And I would say good friends and strong allies. But lots of mistakes were made back then, among them America's not giving proper recognition to how important Filipinos were in the defeat of the Spanish forces in the Philippines."

"So then what happened, Teacher? I mean, after things settled down between the US and the Filipinos who fought them after the treaty?"

"In a way, I suppose you can say that the US tried to Americanize the population through public education, teaching of the English language, and laying the groundwork for a democratic form of government. About 500 teachers from the US were recruited in 1901 to teach in the Philippines. They became known at the Thomasites."

"Thomasites? Why were they called Thomasites?"

"Had to do with the name of the ship they traveled on, the USAT Thomas. USAT stood for United States Army Transport."

"Hm. Makes sense," said the Kano.

"The US also provided educational grants for Filipinos to come to America to study and earn a college degree. They were known as *pensionados*. In 1903, the first group of students came to California."

"Thomasites and pensionados. Check and check," said the Kano as he made two air checks again with his right index finger.

"About 100,000 Filipinos came to Hawaii and the mainland during the next 30 years. The first group was known as the *sakadas* and were from various areas of the Philippines. The second group to come were called *wenmanongs*, and they were mostly from the Ilocos region."

"Like when men were men and when men were manongs?

"No, it's one word, *wenmanongs*," said the Teacher. "Wenmanongs. In the Ilocano language it means 'older brother.'"

"I always wanted to be an older brother."

"In Tagalog, that's called *kuya*."

"*That* is called 'cool ya'?"

"Kuya. Yes, coo-yah."

"Why is *that* called kuya?"

"Uh, I don't know, it just is," said the Teacher.

"What about older brother; what's that called in Tagalog?"

"*Kuya*, I just told you."

"I thought kuya was *that*," said the Kano.

"Uh-huh," said the Teacher.

"So, kuya means 'that' and kuya means 'older brother' too?" asked the Kano.

"I see the confusion. We're actually talking about two different words. In Tagalog, kuya means 'older brother.' And the Tagalog word *na* translates into the English word 'that.'"

"Cool-ya. I mean cool."

"Anyway, these early Filipino immigrants were young men with only minimal education, and they mostly found work in the pineapple and sugar cane fields of Hawaii."

"Pineapples and sugar? Sounds like sweet work, Teacher."

"More like sweat work. It was brutal, toiling in the hot fields for 10 or 12 hours a day, for $20 a month. And the Filipinos were considered the lowest on the ethnic ladder—which means they made less than the Chinese and the Japanese for the same work."

"Not fair!"

"And if it wasn't working in the fields, they still remained on the bottom of the labor tree—they made the beds in hotels, worked in restaurants, were busboys or bellhops, or did physical labor."

"Where did they live? On the sugar plantations?"

"There was housing for workers, but that wasn't fair either. These dorms were dirty, crowded, and generally unsanitary—and, the worker's wages were deducted to pay for it! If there was any upside, the dorms were segregated by ethnicity, so they at least shared a common language and culture."

"Did the Filipino immigrants only work in Hawaii?" asked the Kano.

"No, some found work on the US mainland, mostly in California."

"I heard Maria say something about Filipinos living in California—that a lot live there."

"That's true, and they can thank these early immigrants who paved the way for them. In those days, Filipinos became the backbone of the California labor force, that's for sure," said the Teacher. "It was grueling work. They started before sunrise, at 4 a.m., and finished when the sun went down. They picked cotton, tomatoes, celery, onions, peas, lettuce, and asparagus. Stoop labor, it was called."

"Stoop labor?" questioned the Kano.

"Yes, stoop labor. I guess it was a pejorative as Filipinos were thought to be ideally suited for this, as they were relatively short and could get down on their hands and knees and do the picking, all day."

"Must have been brutal on their backs."

"It was, but they had to keep pushing on. None of today's medicines, back braces, heating cushions, or lotions to ease the pain. No wife to come home to for comfort or a home-cooked meal. It was a difficult life."

"Certainly sounds like it, Teacher."

"These fields, they were brutally hot, maybe even hotter than in the Philippines. The dust, and the dirt, it was everywhere; you couldn't escape from it. And it was made worse by the California winds blowing it all up in their eyes, and ears, and noses. All day long. And sweat. Sweat dripping from their foreheads into their eyes, mixing with the dust and dirt. And that sweat dripped down their backs too, creating a constant itch that no scratch could satisfy. All day long. And then, after a brutal 12 hours of backbreaking, painful work, they went back to living quarters that were run-down, hot, cramped, and basically squalid. There were long lines to take a bath. Five to ten people would bathe before the water was changed. And every night was the same: They rested their worn-out bodies for the next day's toil, while aching, literally aching, for their family, thousands of miles away, back home in the Philippines."

The Kano let out a long sigh. He didn't say anything for a few moments; he didn't have to. Wanting to know more, he asked, "Did the Filipinos find work in other areas of the country, or was it mostly in Hawaii and California?"

"A lot were recruited for work in the salmon canneries in Alaska. Very physical labor there too—mostly loading and unloading trucks and gutting and cleaning the salmon, from 6 a.m. to 6 p.m.. It was a long day filled with the smell of fish and scales. These Filipinos became known as *Alaskeros*."

"Alaskeros," repeated the Kano, somewhat disengaged from his own thoughts. "Teacher, you still seem a little sad, telling me about all of this… like you're holding something back. What is it?"

"Kano, it's hard to grasp what these Filipinos went through 100 years ago, when our only context is seeing how successful Filipino immigrants to the US are today. They're highly educated, and the majority are professionals— doctors, nurses, lawyers, engineers, teachers, medical techs, dentists, entrepreneurs, pharmacists, business executives, and computer specialists. They have strong families and a strong faith and are highly adept in our customs and language. I can go on and on."

"Please do, Teacher."

"Yes, so it's hard to understand the serious discrimination against Filipinos back then. It pains me to say it, but it's true."

"How? Tell me."

"Filipinos were seen as outsiders, and I suppose that's not surprising, since they weren't born here. But times were tough, especially during the depression, so these immigrants were competing with white men for jobs—and that bred resentment. Filipino men became the focus of pointed discrimination and open hatred. They were barred from certain kinds of occupations, or from entering restaurants and other kinds of establishments," said the Teacher.

"That's terrible, just terrible."

"If they were allowed in a movie theatre, they had to sit in segregated section. And, this is really horrible, Kano—many hotels, restaurants, and swimming pools bore signs that read 'Positively No Filipinos Allowed!' Can you imagine that?"

"I... I can't. Teacher, I just can't. Horrible. I'm speechless."

"These men lived a desperate and disenfranchised existence. They were so lonely, painfully lonely, and became socially and psychologically isolated in a new and strange land. In the absence of Filipino women, and female companionship in general, they gave up on the idea of establishing a family. They were seen, and saw themselves, as family-less men."

"Teacher, that's so sad, since these men had such a deep-rooted longing to be part of a family. And, many, I'm sure, were working here to support families they did have back home. Did some eventually return?" asked the Kano.

"I suppose some did, but mostly, no. No. Their money didn't go far. Their employers took advantage of them, overcharging for lodging or not paying them a full week's pay. And what little was left, they frittered away in pool rooms, smoke-filled bars, gambling dens, or dance halls."

"Teacher, if they didn't have much money, why would they kind of throw it away in places like that?"

"Again, the Filipino's existence here as a laborer, far away from home, was miserable. Just miserable. And lonely. I can't emphasize enough just how lonely he was. These places became a much-needed escape—a place to wind down, and enjoy a few fleeting moments of leisure. It was unstructured time with no demands, no dust, no scorching sun or screeching steam whistles dictating their every move."

"Teacher, I never realized, I mean…." The Kano sighed. "I just… I wasn't aware."

"Kano, it's understandable. The struggles black Americans have faced are well known, and most people have some sense of the discrimination that Chinese immigrants, particularly railroad workers, faced in the 1850s. Anti-Irish sentiment wasn't uncommon in America at this time either, and I think people generally have heard about the 'No Irish Need Apply' signs that dotted the landscape," said the Teacher.

"But Filipinos, the Filipino struggle in America, it doesn't seem to be well known. Just look at me, I'm guilty of not knowing anything about it," said the Kano.

"The unfortunate tag of invisibility, as it's been called. Well, you know something about it now. That's why I said earlier, I owe all of these early Filipino immigrants such a debt of gratitude. Here's something else to think about— marriage. We take marriage, getting married, I mean, more or less for granted. Wouldn't you say?" asked the Teacher.

"Uh, yes, I suppose."

"Well, during these times of early Filipino immigration to the US, a dozen states had laws outlawing marriages between whites and Filipinos. Can you believe that? Miscegenation laws they were called. Although many states had laws banning interracial marriage generally, in some places, there was animosity, maybe even resentment, toward Filipino men."

"Resentment toward Filipino men? Why do you say that, Teacher?"

"Well, unlike men from China, Japan, or Korea, Filipino men sought out the companionship of American women, who, likewise, were attracted and interested in them. Filipino men were familiar with western culture, educated in American schools, and able to speak English. Despite the discrimination, they saw themselves more as Americans than as foreigners. And I don't think it hurt that, when the weekend came, they were sharp dressers and great dancers!"

"It's just... so hard to imagine. When did it end? When did things get better for these Filipinos?"

"After World War II, that's when things starting getting much better," said the Teacher.

"Finally!"

"Filipinos who served in the US Armed Forces were granted citizenship, and because of the 1945 War Brides Act they could bring their spouses and children."

"That's an act that deserves an encore."

"That's right, and the encore was in 1946 when the Philippines became an independent nation, and those Filipinos in the US had the right to become naturalized citizens, vote, and own land."

"Standing ovation," said the Kano as he stood up from his chair, clapping, to make the point. "Teacher, I realize I had no part in that history, I mean, I wasn't even born; but I feel terrible, just terrible."

"I'm glad you feel empathy," said the Teacher, "because for all the insensitivity you've shown Maria, this tells me that you do care, that knowing something about these early struggles has moved you, has made a difference."

"For all I know, Maria's relatives could have been part of those early waves of Filipino immigration to the US. If they were, I owe them, big time."

"Whether they were or were not, it doesn't really matter. These immigrants paved the way for all the Filipinos who would follow—and achieve levels of success, respect, status, and comfort in America that those who came first could never even dream of," said the Teacher.

"Teacher, this history, this story… it needs to be told."

"Well, I'm telling you. You can tell others. And hopefully you'll be stirred to learn more. For sure, study Carlos Bulosan, a self-educated Filipino immigrant who was an early organizer in the labor movement. Through his writing, he gave a voice to countless, struggling Filipino workers, like the ones I described before. There's a history here that's needs to be told, Kano—why don't you be among those who are telling it?"

"I will Teacher, I will."

"Teacher?"

"Yes Kano, what is it?" replied the Teacher.

"You know what just happened, right? I mean, I'm not dreaming right now, am I? We are back on this deserted beach again?"

"Yes. Yes, that' right. The setting provides a fantastic backdrop, doesn't it?" asked the Teacher.

"I suppose so. Is it going to happen now?"

"Do you mean our Mr. Miyagi and Daniel *Karate Kid* moment? Where the teacher imparts knowledge and wisdom to the student, amidst sounds of the tide washing ashore and a flute ensemble playing in the background?"

"Uh, yes, I suppose. But I thought you couldn't control anything, that things just happened," said the Kano. "How can you make us poof onto a beach?"

"That's true about not being able to control anything, but when I think about something quite a bit, like the beach training scene from the *Karate Kid* movie starring Ralph Macchio and Pat Morita, well, sometimes it can happen."

"Okay, fine. But this saltwater air is making me hungry. Are we doing the lumpy thing again?"

"Lumpia! Kano, it's not hard to pronounce. Just use the old rhyming trick. Remember that lumpia rhymes with, uh… lumpia rhymes with… uh, lumpia. Lumpia. Just say lumpia!"

"Lumpia rhymes with lumpia? Okay…," said the Kano with a hint of sarcasm.

"Let's focus, Kano. Have you developed a greater understanding and appreciation today for the Filipino culture and experience?"

"I have Teacher, I really have. I didn't know anything about Filipino immigration into the US. Didn't even think about it. Guess I sort of took it for granted. You know, it's pretty common to see Filipino people around, especially in New Jersey. But like you said, what the early immigrants went through, the suffering they endured to pave the way for those that followed—it's just remarkable."

"Yes, it certainly is. I'm glad to hear you recognize that," said the Teacher.

"I'm also kind of shocked to hear that some of this migration to the US can be traced back 500 years ago, to the Manila-Acapulco trade route. And, that the US only paid $20 million dollars to purchase the Philippines from Spain as part of the 1898 Treaty of Paris."

"Go on."

"The Thomasites and pensionados, and, oh, the hard, harsh labor the Filipino immigrants faced on the pineapple plantations in Hawaii and in the fields of California, picking cotton, tomatoes, peas and asparagus—in brutal conditions. But I suppose even worse was the discrimination they faced in being Filipinos at that time in America."

"What stood out as most troubling for you to learn about, Kano?

"The signs. The signs that were posted at some hotels and other public places that said 'Positively No Filipinos Allowed.' That tore at me, and I'm not even Filipino."

"And, knowing what these Filipinos endured— discrimination, brutal working conditions, and unbearable loneliness—if you could ask them, was it worth it? Was every bead of sweat, every insult, every hour of so called 'stoop labor'—if they could now see the level of achievement, respect, status, and inclusion that Filipinos in America today enjoy, what would they say?" asked the Teacher.

"I'm quite sure they would say yes. Yes, it was worth it. And, they'd say it with a smile."

"Very good Kano, very good. You have earned another lumpia shanghai. There will be more—here." As the Teacher gave away the tasty morsel, the Kano lost his balance, for he quickly realized that he, and the Teacher, were standing on wooden stumps, jutting out from the beach.

"Teacher, I almost fell, there's no room on this stump," said the Kano, steadying himself while biting into the lumpia shanghai. "What were you thinking about?"

"Since I'm on the thought plane of the *Karate Kid*, you and I are now practicing on wooden stumps, like Mr. Miyagi and Daniel did."

"Teacher, if you can think and make stuff happen, I'd prefer to be standing on a giant lumpia jutting up from the beach, not wooden stumps."

"Why do you say that, Kano?"

"Then, I can eat my way to the ground, instead of eating the ground, which almost just happened!"

CHAPTER 5
HOME, SWEET HOME

It was 5:00 a.m., and like the previous two mornings, the Kano's alarm clock began buzzing loudly. He groaned and knocked the clock off the nightstand in an attempt to stop it. As he pulled the covers over his head to hide underneath them in the darkness, the Teacher appeared in the room.

"Good morning Kano," said the Teacher.

"What's so good about it?"

"What's so *gude* about it, you ask?" said the Teacher.

"Yea, sure, guuude. What's so guuude about it?" asked the Kano sarcastically.

"It's gude, because I, your teacher, am a fan of Vince Lombardi, the legendary head coach of the Green Bay Packers."

"Uh-huh."

"And you know what he said? Lombardi said you've got to become brilliant at the basics. And you, Kano, need more instruction in the basics."

"The basics?"

"Yes, the basics. I call it Filipino 101," said the Teacher.

"Filipino 101? Sounds like Algebra 101. I wasn't very good in Algebra, Teacher."

"Kano, you won't have to memorize any algebraic equations, but you need to understand how faith, family, food—and Lola, form the bedrock of Filipino culture."

"Faith, family, food… and Lola? Teacher, can't we be a bit more alliterative here? How about faith, family, food, and festive?"

"Kano, we're not playing a word-find game, although 'festive' is an adjective that describes the Filipino people. For purposes of being culturally acclimated, understanding the Lola is of great importance in your training."

"Acclimated? That's a big word, Teacher, like polynomial. I thought Filipino 101 wasn't going to be like Algebra."

"Kano, by *culturally acclimated* I mean adopting, understanding, and appreciating the Filipino culture."

"Okay, but how long does all this take? I want to win Maria's heart now. Don't get me wrong, I'm down with faith, family, food, and festive lolas; but, Teacher, when does this training end? When will you shanghai another lumpia in your hand?"

"To the kitchen, Kano."

The Teacher went to the flip chart and wrote *Home, Sweet Home*. "Today, we are going to pay a visit to a Filipino family—the Mendozas, and you will learn many things. But for now, let's start with some discussion of the Lola." The

Teacher flipped to a blank sheet and in the center drew a face with the word *Lola* above it.

"Uh, Teacher, is that picture supposed to be a lola?"

"Are you hinting that my drawing skills need some work, Kano?"

"No, I'm not hinting about it."

"Kano, I wasn't an art major. Now, the Lola is the keeper of history, traditions, and even superstitions, which you'll learn a whole lot more about as your training continues."

"Uh-huh."

"The Lola is so important to the Filipino family. She is full of love, especially for her grandchildren. Such a wonderful soul. She's always worried that the guests haven't eaten enough, whether it's her party or someone else's."

"You're describing Maria's mother to a *T*," said the Kano.

"The Lola is the bridge to the past. She's especially important for the new generation who weren't born in the Philippines. Of course, this extends to the Lolo, or grandfather, as well."

"At Maria's housewarming party, I saw several couples who I think were the lolos and lolas," said the Kano.

"Yes, a party is not a party without your lola or lolo there," said the Teacher. "Or someone else's."

"Someone else's?"

"Yes, in Filipino culture, someone considered a relative isn't always blood related, and genealogy can be, well, a bit creative at times," said the Teacher.

"So, if I marry Maria, not only can I call her grandmother Lola, but other random people as well?"

"I think I'd follow the lead of those around you, but, the terms *lola* and *lolo* can sometimes be used for a female or male who's older, or I should say, old enough. In the Filipino culture, it is considered as a sign of respect to the elders," said the Teacher.

"Respect for elders is important," said the Kano.

"It is. Filipino children are taught from birth how to say *po* and *opo* to teach them as early as possible how to properly respect their elders. These words are used to show respect to people who are older. Even adults will be criticized for not using them when speaking with their parents or people older than them," said the Teacher.

"Po, Opo. Check-po," said the Kano, making an air check again with his index finger.

"It's not unusual for grandparents to live with family members rather than on their own. Did we talk about *utang na loob*?"

"You tang uh-oh? No, I don't remember," said the Kano. "But now that you mention Tang, I could use a refreshing drink."

"Kano, focus. I didn't say 'Tang,' I said *utang na loob*! It's the principle of reciprocity, and includes repaying those who have treated you well. It can be the younger generation's way of repaying their parents for the care they received as children."

"Not only does that sound nice, it seems appropriate," said the Kano.

"At the same time, the grandparents make significant contributions to the household, often providing child care for their grandchildren. This can be particularly important for some families that have a parent working abroad, and lolas and lolos often step in to help fill the gap left by a parent's absence," said the Teacher.

"I want a lola!" said the Kano.

"Another reason you'll see grandparents living with their children is when a Filipino family migrates to the US, they usually live together because the family is such an important source of emotional, moral, and economic support."

"Was it that way for your wife? I mean your asawa?"

"Yes, hers is the iconic immigrant story. Her oldest sister, Connie, or Ate, first came to the United States and began the petition process to—"

"You don't remember?" interrupted the Kano.

"Remember what?"

"Which sister," said the Kano.

"What are you talking about?"

"Which sister came to the US?"

"Yes, Connie, or Ate, came to the U.S first," said the Teacher.

"Yes, which one was it?" asked the Kano.

"Kano, you're testing my patience. What are you talking about?"

"I just want to get the story straight. Let me ask it this way. Who in your wife's family came first to America?"

"Okay, sure. It was her oldest sister, Connie, or Ate," said the Teacher.

"Teacher, it's okay if you don't remember which one," said the Kano. "The memory is the first thing to go when you're old."

"My memory is just fine! And I'm not old! What do you mean which one?" yelled the Teacher. "What are you talking about? She can only have one oldest sister!"

Emphasizing the names in a slow, exaggerated tone, the Kano asked, "Teacher, was it her *oldest* sister, Connie, or was it her *other oldest* sister, Atay, who first came to America?"

"Ahh, now I see," said the Teacher. "Your kano-ness is showing. As we say in Tagalog, you're acting a bit *antipatiko*."

"I don't think I like the sound of that—at least not the way you're saying it," said the Kano. "I'd like it better if it sounded more like antipasto. I'm famished; how about you?"

"Antipasto means you're acting like a smart alek," said the Teacher. "Er, I mean antipatiko. Antipatiko means 'smart alek.'"

"A smart alek? Teacher, I'm just trying to understand your story."

"Maybe, but since you interrupted and didn't wait for more context, you processed what I said, not with a Filipino spirt, but with an arrogant kano-ness."

"I'm sorry, Teacher."

"Patience and an open mind will go far to improve your relationship with Maria, and her family. Not to mention you will gain a greater appreciation of the Filipino culture and way of life."

"Please, go on," said the Kano.

"The term *Ate* is a respectful way to address one's oldest sister. So, my asawa's eldest sister, Connie, is also called Ate."

"I'm feeling pretty embarrassed," said the Kano.

"You should. Now, back to the story. Connie, or Ate, first came to the United States to work and establish herself so that she could start the process to bring the rest of the family here."

"Did everybody come?" asked the Kano.

"Just about. A sister and brother, Lisa and Joel, wanted to stay home in the Philippines, but everyone else eventually found themselves living in New York City, in a small two-bedroom apartment in what's called Stuyvesant Town. With Lola and Lolo, I think there were nine people living together in that small space."

"Wow, that's amazing—and Ate Connie paved the way to America for her whole family!"

"She did, thankfully—because they all wanted to come to America for a better life too—they believed in the American Dream. And I'm happy to say, they have all shared in it," said the Teacher.

"Sadly, there are people who are born right here in America who don't believe in the dream," said the Kano.

"We need hard-working immigrants, like Filipinos, to remind them of their birthright."

"Sure do. I think my wife's family is typical of so many immigrants who come to America for a better life—they are willing to sacrifice and do the hard work to achieve it. And for some, like my sister-in-law Ethel, the hard work also supports family still in the Philippines, who dream of coming to America too. So there's a great appreciation for our country, and probably why Filipino immigrants are quite patriotic. It's not uncommon to find them serving in the US military. In fact, my brothers-in-law Leleng, Ibet, and Paul all served."

"Three of your wife's brothers—all served the United States military? You're right, that is one patriotic family, Teacher. I, uh, I would have definitely joined the Marines, but you know, I've got this flat-feet thing going on."

"Some Filipino immigrants have served with great distinction, too, Kano, like Eleanor Concepcion Mariano. She is the first Filipino to become an admiral in the US Navy and the first female physician to serve as the official doctor for the President of the United States."

"Oh my, that's something. When was that?"

"She was the White House physician from 1992 to 2001," said the Teacher.

"Must be a pretty hard road to get there."

"Nothing worthwhile is easy, Kano." "She actually came from a naval family and was born in 1955 at the former Clark Air Base in Angeles City, Pampanga, in the Philippines."

"Was her father transferred to the United States at some point?"

"Yes, when she was just a little girl. She was an excellent student, the valedictorian of her high school class."

"I'm sure the Mariano family's refrigerator was covered with glowing report cards."

"She received her medical degree from the Uniformed Services University School of Medicine in Bethseda, Maryland, and her first active duty assignment in the navy was on a destroyer, the *USS Prairie*."

"She's an inspiration for all Filipinos," remarked the Kano.

"Not just Filipinos. She's an inspiration for anyone," said the Teacher.

"So true."

"Well Kano, I think it's about time we make that visit to the Mendoza family."

"Can I brush my teeth first?" asked the Kano. "And, maybe you can make some breakfast for your famished student?"

"Hmm, not a bad idea. Tell you what, I'll pop out and get some tocino and pandesal, and also some Spam and…"

"Pop out? Did you say 'Spam'?"

"Yes, I don't think you have any Spam here," said the Teacher.

"Whatcha gonna do, channel your inner Spam?"

"No," said the Teacher. "I'll just go to the convenience store and get some."

"How can you do that? You don't have a car."

"Remember, I'm a ghost!" With that and a laugh, poof! The Teacher disappeared.

Later, the delicious, lingering smell of the tocino remained in the kitchen, despite its having been entirely eaten. Clearly satisfied, the Kano pushed his chair from the table, leaned back, placed his hands on his stomach and said, "Hmm, that tocino was good, Teacher. I mean masarap."

"I'm glad you liked it."

"I'm confused. One moment you're right in front of me, and in another moment you're gone. Then, I find myself at the kitchen table and there's a mountain of tocino and pandesal and Spam in front of me. But Teacher, I don't have tocino or pandesal, or even Spam, in the house! And, no stores are open at this early hour, except the 7-Eleven, which I'm certain doesn't carry a Filipino line of food, or they'd call it seben–eleben."

"Seben-eleben? Kano, you haven't earned the right to be playful with the Filipino accent," said the Teacher a little sternly. "When you truly love the culture, customs, and people—when you 'get it'—you can, along with Filipinos themselves, have some fun with this. But right now, don't even go there!"

"You're right. I'm sorry, Teacher."

"Anyway, I got the tocino, pandesal and Spam at the *tindahan*. *Tindahan* means 'a store' in Tagalog. I went to a Filipino store."

"Sorry Teacher, this is not computing. I'm not aware of any 24-hour Filipino grocery stores around here. Where did you go? You say you're not a ghost, but you can just go poof here and poof there and fly around and go to places and—"

"I don't have wings, Kano," said the Teacher as he turned around. "See? And, though I may poof, I don't fly around. Remember, I'm not bound by space... or time."

"Well, what about money? Are you bound by money? You don't have any money, do you?"

"Why do I need money?"

"To buy the tocino, pandesal, and Spam!"

"I didn't buy it," said the Kano.

"What! What kind of teacher are you? How can you steal? What kind of example are you setting for me? I'm young and impressionable!" the Kano lamented.

"Kano! *Alala kulugo*. You're such a worry wart," said the Teacher. "I didn't steal anything. You're forgetting that when you're with me, we're functioning in a different dimension."

"A different dimension? Like the Twilight Zone?"

"Something like that," said the Teacher.

"Teacher, seriously, I must know—since you don't have any money, how did you get all this food for free?"

"You've heard of virtual reality?"

"Yes," said the Kano.

"And bitcoin?"

"Yes, the virtual money that's used on the internet. Why?"

"Let's just say there's no need for you to count calories," said the Teacher.

"You mean... my breakfast, it wasn't... wasn't real?" asked the Kano

"It depends on your definition of real, but yes."

"Uy."

"Kano, enough with this breakfast talk. We have important matters to attend to."

"Sounds good to me, Teacher," said the Kano as he started to get up from the kitchen table. "Well, I'd wash the dishes, but since they're in another dimension—"

"Actually, they're not in another dimension. They're in the sink. And they're dirty," said the Teacher.

"Teacher! Why can my food be in another dimension, but not the dirty dishes?"

"Kano, even the Twilight Zone didn't make sense at times. This Filipino Zone we're in now is even more *loko-loko*," he said as he passed the Kano a scrub brush.

With a slight look of annoyance, the Kano began washing. When he finished, the Teacher asked, "Kano, are you familiar with 'A Christmas Story?'"

"You mean Scrooge?"

"Yes, Ebenezer Scrooge. You remember what happened when he drifted off to sleep, don't you?"

"Teacher, are you saying that I'm an old, greedy, mean millionaire who needs to be taught a lesson by spirits of the night? I don't mind the millionaire part, but I'm rather young, and pretty nice too, don't you think?"

"Yes, you're rather young."

"And pretty nice? Wouldn't you say? Nice. Nice? Wouldn't you say? Earth to Teacher. Teacher!"

"Fine, fine, you're nice, but you are not focused—you're all over the place. You must stay focused on your training if you expect to win Maria's heart."

"Okay, Okay, I understand. I'm ready. Now, tell me about this Scrooge thing."

"I was attempting to make an analogy between—"

"Is that a Tagalog word?"

"Is what a Tagalog word?"

"Alogy. Is *alogy* a Tagalog word? Sounds like it… because if it is, I'm ready. Just tell me what it means, and, I'll store it right here in the old vault," said the Kano, tapping his forehead with an index finger. "Yessiree, I'm focused, I'm ready, I'm—"

"Not an English major. Kano, I didn't say 'alogy,' I said 'analogy.' And, it's an English word! It means a comparison of two things, to help explain something."

"Oh. Uh, okay. Well, I'm still ready, yessiree, ready to store it all in the old vault," said the Kano as he began tapping his forehead again.

"The point I was trying to make is similar to how Scrooge was taken by a spirit to a particular place and time; I can do the same with you."

"Cool. And you're not a ghost, right?"

"Yes, I'm not a ghost! Or is it no, I'm not a ghost. In either case, because of my Filipino spirit, I can transport you with me to places or moments in time where you can learn more about Filipinos and their culture."

"Transport? How does this work, exactly?" asked the Kano.

"Transport? Kind of like it happened in *The Wizard of Oz*—another analogy Kano—ah-nahl-oh-gee—except you don't need to wear red shoes to get there," laughed the Teacher.

"Uh, okay...."

"Don't tell me you haven't seen *The Wizard of Oz*. Anyway, you'll need to stand up straight, close your eyes, and instead of clicking your heels and saying 'there's no place like home,' you'll repeat *'Ang Aking Espiritu Ay Filipino'* after me," said the Teacher. 'Ang Aking Espiritu Ay Filipino.' Three times."

"Huh? You want me to say 'I'm a king of the Filipino spirits?' Are you sure? A king? That seems rather boastful, don't you think? I'm new to this. And what will that do, anyway?" asked the Kano.

"No, no, no. This has nothing to do with you being a king of anyone or anything! Ang Aking Espiritu Ay Filipino is Tagalog for 'My Spirit is Filipino.' Saying this, with genuine feeling, will help activate your inner Filipino, which will be important in getting back Maria, not to mention the ability to transport. You have a lot to learn to win her over, Kano. Besides, repeating Ang Aking Espiritu Ay Filipino is required to become invisible and be a fly on the wall, which we'll be doing," said the Teacher.

"What, a fly on the wall? Invisible?" asked the Kano. "You said you weren't a ghost!"

"Whenever you're ready."

"I'll never be ready for this," said the Kano.

"Then you'll never be ready to fight for Maria's love. Yesterday you were Mr. OA, ready to scale Mt. Pinatubo while it oozed with lava to prove to Maria how you oozed with love for her. Now, you're afraid to become invisible and continue your training in The Way of the Filipino?"

"I'm not afraid, just a little, well, nervous. Do I have to hold my breath? I probably should avoid that. I think I have asthma. Or maybe it's emphysema. Or COPD."

"Kano, are you in, or are you out?"

"Uh, I'm in."

"Okay, then repeat after me, Ang Aking Espiritu Ay Filipino," said the Teacher.

"I'm the king—uh-oh, sorry. Ang Aking Espiritu Ay Filipino," said the Kano.

They repeated it together, two more times. Ang Aking Espiritu Ay Filipino. Ang Aking Espiritu Ay Filipino.

Suddenly, everything went silent and dark. And then poof! They found themselves on the front lawn of a neatly manicured, two-story colonial home in a nice residential neighborhood.

"Can you see me?" asked the Kano with eyes tightly closed and a bit shaken. "I can't see you! I can't see you! Does Espirtu-ing make you go blind? Oh no, I'll never see Maria's beautiful face again."

"Kano, of course I can see you," replied the Teacher. "And you can see me—if you just open your eyes!"

Cautiously opening one eye first and then the other, the Kano cried out, "Teacher, I never thought I'd say that you are the beauty in the eye of this beholder."

"Well, don't say it. It's disturbing."

"Look, a family is pulling into the driveway in a minivan. And they are Filipino!" said the Kano eagerly.

"What did you expect? An Irish family? Of course they are Filipino," said the Teacher. "It's some members of the Mendoza family. Have you forgotten why I popped out of nowhere into your life?"

"Uh, yeah, sure; I just got excited," said the Kano.

"Looks like Dad is driving. His name is Ramon, and he's 51. In the passenger seat is his oldest daughter, Peaches, who's 22. The other two children in the middle seats are his daughter Lilibeth, who's 20, and his son Tres, who's 12. Already at home are his wife, Floribeth, who is 46, and their

8-year-old son, Adonis, as well as the in-laws and a few other relatives who stopped in for a visit."

"Peaches? Tres? Adonis?"

"Yes, it's not all that unusual, if you're Filipino, to use the name of fruits to name your child. Or numbers. Or to add parts of names together. Or to just be creative generally. The sky's the limit."

"How come you know everyone's name?"

"If I can poof you from one place to another before you can blink, do you even need to ask?"

"I guess you're right."

"Okay. Well, let's take in our surroundings, so that I may start to teach you The Way of the Filipino," said the Teacher.

"Ready," said the Kano.

"Let's walk toward the front door. Ahh, smell those roses? It's not uncommon for the Filipino to have rose bushes in front of the house."

"A rose by any other name, even my Maria, would still smell as sweet," said the Kano, clearly being OA. "Besides, I think that somehow, her first middle name, or maybe it's her second middle name, or it could even be her mother's maiden name, or a combination of the using a vowel from her first name, three consonants from her second name and, or... uh... anyway, I think Rose is there somewhere."

The Teacher and the Kano approached the front door. They didn't ring the bell or knock on the door but simply walked through it.

"Woooooh, what just happened?" asked the Kano.

"Our Filipino spirits—or, I should say, my Filipino spirit—isn't confined by the physical world, nor is yours when you're with me. We can go practically anywhere we want to, like walking right through this front door. But, there are a few restrictions," said the Teacher.

"Like what?"

"Like where you'll find a *tabo*," said the Teacher.

"Tebow?" asked the Kano. "Are you referring to Tim Tebow, the NFL quarterback? Or, sometimes NFL quarterback? Or kind of baseball player? What's he got to do with any of this?"

"No, not Tebow, Kano, tabo."

"Tebow tabo? What's that?"

"No, not Tebow tabo, just tabo."

"What about Tim?" asked the Kano.

"Tim who?"

"Tebow."

"No, it's tabo," said the Teacher.

"Tim Tabo? Who's that, a Filipino I should know?"

"No, not Tim Tabo. Just tabo. Tabo!" yelled the Teacher.

"Oh, do you mean that dipper thing in the bathroom that is used to clean and freshen one up after, you know, mother nature calls?" asked the Kano. "Yes, I know all about the tabo, Maria gave me the inside scoop about it at the party."

"The inside scoop?"

"By the way, talking about Tim Tabo, er, I mean Tim Tebow, the former NFL quarterback, I read that he grew up in the Philippines. Is that true?" asked the Kano.

If Tim Tebow was a tabo

"Yes, his parents were doing missionary work, and he was born there. In Makati, if I'm not mistaken. He spent the first few years of his life in the Philippines, before the family moved back to the United States. I'm pretty sure that the Christian ministry his father started back then still continues today," said the Teacher. "Now, let's get back to our surroundings. Having just walked through the front door, we are now standing in the foyer. Tell me what you see."

"Well, it would be hard not to mention the piles of slippers, mountains of them, really, here on the foyer floor. We only saw a few people in the minivan. Are there dozens more people living here? I mean, does everybody have their own eight pairs of slippers?" asked the Kano.

"First, they are not called slippers. They are *tsinelas*," said the Teacher.

"Chinelas?" repeated the Kano.

"Yes, tsinelas. These are fixtures at a Filipino household. There will always be more tsinelas than the number of people living in the home."

"Why?" asked the Kano.

"For guests. Because upon entrance into a Filipino home, one takes off their shoes, and—whaaaaaaat? Why are you still wearing your shoes?!" shouted the Teacher. "Get them off immediately!"

"Okay, they're off. Sorry," said the Kano, a little surprised by the Teacher's reaction.

"Uy, why is your big toe sticking out?"

"Because I have a hole in my sock."

"Yes, I see that. By why do you have a hole in your sock?"

"The threads tore apart."

"Yes, I know the threads tore apart, but why do you— oh, forget it. Just make sure you wear socks without holes when you visit Maria. And cut your toenails."

"Teacher, you're embarrassing me!"

"Okay, enough of this. Put on a pair of tsinelas."

"I thought we were ghosts; why do I need slippers?" asked the Kano.

"How many times do I have to tell you, Kano, we are not ghosts! And they are tsinelas! You are in training. You must accustom yourself to The Way of the Filipino. And one of those ways is respecting their customs and traditions. Like putting on tsinelas. Besides, it makes for a much cleaner home than the American way of walking around in dirty shoes."

Putting on his tsinelas, the Kano looked at the Teacher and giggled. Pointing to his feet he remarked, "Teacher, your chinelas look kind of girly, you know, pink with a fluffy strap and all. You can do better than that, can't you?"

"Yes, you're right, I can." Poof! The pink and fluffy tsinelas were now on the Kano.

"Teacher!"

As the Teacher slipped on another pair, the Kano said, "I hope Maria will appreciate what I'm going through to win her heart. Pink slippers… er, chinelas. Is there anything I should know about these?"

"I'm glad you're interested in something more than how you look, which, by the way, needs some work. Your clothes seem a bit wrinkled, don't you think? Why don't you use some starch the next time you iron?"

"Starch? Iron?" I know those words aren't Tagalog, Teacher, but I don't know what they mean, if you know what I mean."

"Unfortunately, yes, I do. Anyway, tsinelas comes from the Spanish word *chinela*, which means a light, low-cut footwear that slips on easily. In the Philippines, or as my asawa says, 'back home,' the tsinela holds an important place. Boys play a game called *tumbang-preso* where they use their tsinelas to hit a can inside a drawn circle. And, there are two towns in the Philippines that have tsinela festivals to showcase their local tsinela industry," said the Teacher.

"Who would have thought a slipper had so much importance?" said the Kano. Seeing his Teacher's face flush, he quickly added, "I mean chinela, chinela!"

"There's another use for the tsinela, beyond footwear or for games," said the Teacher.

"What's that?"

"Just ask any Filipino child who doesn't obey his parents or grandparents. He can tell you!" said the Teacher with a laugh.

"Teacher, I hear something in the family room. Can we go over there?" asked the Kano.

"Yes, and as we walk through the formal living room, tell me what you observe."

"The room is very clean, and it smells good," said the Kano.

"Yes, very typical of the Filipino home, clean and wonderful smelling. Go on," suggested the Teacher.

"The couches are covered in plastic. Even the lampshades!" said the Kano. "And some of the plastic is covered in plastic. Uh, I also see lots of mirrors, and some plastic runners over the carpeted areas," said the Kano.

"Good. What else?" asked the Teacher.

"What's that on the wall? Right there, a wood carving with people dancing and holding long sticks," said the Kano.

"Yes, that carving depicts the *tinikling*. It's a traditional Philippine dance that originated in the Spanish colonial era," said the Teacher.

"Why are there sticks?" asked the Kano.

"They're not sticks, exactly—they're bamboo poles. Two people beat, tap, and slide the bamboo poles on the ground while one dancer, and sometime more than one, steps over and in between in a dance, while music plays," said the Teacher.

"Sort of like jump rope, like double-dutch," said the Kano.

"Yes, in a way," said the Teacher. "It's regarded by some as the national dance of the Philippines."

"Why is it called the teeny tiny can?" asked the Kano. "I don't see any teeny tiny cans, just sticks."

"Tinikling," said the Teacher. "Tin-ee-kling."

"Ahh, tin-ee-kling," said the Kano. "Tin-ee-kling."

"Yes, good. It originated in the Visayan Islands, and the dancers there imitated the tikling bird. These birds show tremendous grace and speed as they walk between grass stems, run over tree branches, or dodge bamboo traps set by farmers."

"Kind of like the Kung Fu master whose style imitates a grasshopper or crane?"

"Yes, something like that."

"It's a funny name, though. Uh-oh, can I say that, you know, or is it insulting, since I'm in training to get my Filipino on?" asked the Kano.

"Sure, it's okay to find names of Filipino things funny or even odd. So long as you are genuinely appreciative and respectful of the culture. Believe me, it's fine. Filipinos are the first to laugh at themselves. It's an endearing quality."

"On the other wall, I see a picture of the Last Supper," said the Kano.

"Yes, having a portrait of the Last Supper is pretty much a given in the Filipino home," said the Teacher. "We have one in ours."

"But why is there a giant spoon and fork on either side of it?" asked the Kano.

"I'm not sure what is more difficult to answer," said the Teacher. "Why there is a giant spoon and fork, or why there isn't a giant knife as well."

"Huh?"

"We'll talk about forks and spoons later, when we see our Filipino family eating," said the Teacher.

"Okay, whatever you say."

"What else do you see?" asked the Teacher.

"I see lots of framed diplomas and plaques. High school diplomas, college degrees, perfect attendance awards from grade school and a no-cavity certificate from the dentist," said the Kano.

"Yes, the Filipino mom is proud to display her children's accomplishments," said the Teacher.

"And there is the infamous karaoke machine," said the Kano.

"No Filipino home would be complete without one," said the Teacher.

"I see a bunch of CDs next to the machine. Looks like disco hits from the '70s."

"Not surprising. What else do you see?" asked the Teacher.

"Is that a Buddha on top of the piano?" asked the Kano. "Isn't Buddha a Chinese God? I thought you told me that most Filipinos are Catholic."

"The laughing Buddha is thought to be a good-luck symbol. You'll hear about lots of other good-luck beliefs, too. Anyway, the Buddha is an influence from Chinese Filipinos, but it's not prayed to, like a statue of a saint, or thought to be miraculous, like the Santo Niño," said the Teacher.

"Santo Niño?" asked the Kano.

"Yes, look in the corner. There's a small shrine set up below the mirror. That statue? It's the Santo Niño de Cebu," said the Teacher.

"Yes, I see it. It's beautiful."

"Santo Niño is the Spanish name for the Christ Child. It's the oldest religious image in the Philippines, brought to the island by Magellan in 1521. He gave it to Queen Juana of Cebu as a baptismal gift. It's thought to be miraculous."

"I think I saw one of these at Maria's house," said the Kano. "Why is it considered miraculous?"

"In 1565, Cebu was set on fire by the Spaniards as punishment for the Cebuanos' rebellion," said the Teacher. "In one of the burned houses, a Spanish soldier found the Santo Niño, in perfect condition. It became the patron saint of the Cebuanos and is venerated by Filipinos everywhere."

Passing by the hutch, the Kano noticed it was filled with beautiful statues. "This is one room I won't be playing ball in," said the Kano.

"A wise decision. Don't play ball in the house, as they say. Those are Lladros, beautiful porcelain statues. You'll be hard pressed to find a Filipino home without them."

Continuing to the family room, the Kano bumped into the Chinese wall screen and stumbled over some small pieces of Chinese furniture and some useless trinkets.

"Kano! Shh."

Peering through the entrance, they saw the Lola, along with her daughter, a few of her grandchildren, and some of the titas, gathered in the family room watching TV.

"Look, look!" said the Lola excitedly, pointing at the TV.

"Ayy!" screamed the daughter.

"Ayy!" screamed the Lola.

"Ayy!" screamed the titas.

"What's happening? Why all the screaming?" asked the Kano. "Has a natural disaster just taken place? Is there some earth-shattering news? Has someone just died?"

"No," said the Teacher. "They just saw a Filipino on TV."

The Kano and the Teacher listened in on the conversation.

"Ma, I think returning the expensive birthday gift that my friend gave me would be very insulting," said Floribeth. "They aren't just shoes, they're Guccis."

"That's Floribeth," said the Teacher. "Remember Ramon, the dad from the minivan? That's his wife."

"Suit yourself," said the Lola. "But don't be surprised if he steps on your toes later. Anyway, those shoes probably didn't cost her too much. They were on sale, so he got a *gude* deal. Plus, she gets another 33.273% off with her employee discount."

"Ma, how come you know everybody's employee discount?"

Ignoring the question, the Lola asked one of the children in the room, who was about six, "Anak, can you ask your lolo if he packed the Cutex for me? I have to polish my nails."

"Uh, is the kid's name A Knock?" asked the Kano. "You told me Filipinos are creative with names. Is A Knock sort of similar? Is that a thing? Names that have to do with gaining entrance to a home?"

"Kano, Lola called that little girl *anak*. Anak is a Tagalog word for 'child.' It can be used for your child or for children in general. It's very common."

"Oh, okay. Innocent mistake, right?" Changing the subject, he asked, "Teacher, I heard the Lola ask for Cutex to polish her nails. Isn't that nail polish remover?"

"It is. But Cutex also makes nail polish," said the Teacher. "And some Filipinas use the term *Cutex* generically to mean 'nail polish,' regardless of the brand."

"Kind of like Kleenex," said the Kano.

The child walked out, down the hallway and into the guest bedroom, to find her lolo. He and a few others were seated on Samsonite folding chairs, playing a game with tiles on an old card table. The Teacher and Kano followed her into the click-clacking sound of the room.

"Teacher, this doesn't look like poker. Or sound like it. What game are they playing?"

"Mahjong," said the Teacher.

"Ma Joe? Is this another name thingy-thing?" asked the Kano. "Okay, which one is Ma Joe: the woman to my right or the man to my left?"

"Kano. Repeat after me: mah-joan-g... mah-joan-g... mah-joan-g."

"Uh-oh, feels like we're going to poof somewhere again. Okay, I'm in," said the Kano. He closed his eyes and repeated "mah-joan-g... .mah-joan-g... my spirit is mah-joan-g."

"Oh, brother," said the Teacher. "Kano! Open your eyes!"

"Huh?"

"Kano, mahjong is a tile-based game that originated in China during the Qing dynasty, in the 18th and 19th centuries, based on popular card games. It's usually played with four people and is a game of skill, strategy, and calculation, but it also involves a degree of chance."

"It may not be poker, but they look as serious as the players in the World Series of Poker," said the Kano.

"Yes, well, the game was imported to the United States in the 1920s. You've heard of Abercrombie and Fitch, I assume?"

"Yes, the retailer. Why?" asked the Kano.

"The first mahjong sets in the US were sold by Abercrombie & Fitch, around 1920. About 12,000, if I'm remembering correctly."

"Really? Wow, who would have thought mahjong and Abercrombie and Fitch shared some common ground," said the Kano.

"In the 1920s, there was a bit of a mahjong fad here in the US. The game became more popular than chess or checkers."

"Fascinating."

Returning to the Lola, the child gave her the Cutex and then joined her cousins. The Lola and her daughter were still conversing.

"Ma," said Floribeth, "I love how you want to teach the children about the old country and our traditions and such, but some of what you tell them is pure superstition."

"Suit yourself. But look at you. What harm was there in waiting until you were one before cutting your hair?"

"Are you implying that because hair from my first haircut, at age one, was placed in some books, I became smart?"

"I have all your report cards. And gold stars. And smiley faces," said the Lola. "You wouldn't even know there was a reprigerator in the kitchen when you were growing up, it was so plastered with all your achievements. You should be more grateful."

"I suppose all the time I spent studying, doing my homework and extra credits, that didn't have anything to do with my good grades? It's just because my hair was in a book?" said the daughter, a bit exasperated.

"I'm sure it helped," said the Lola.

"Lola," giggled Marisol, one of the grandchildren. "I was so *kalbo*, there was nothing to put into a book."

"Kalbo?" asked the Kano.

"Bald."

"Can I still be smart, Lola?" she asked.

"Yes, just don't sit on your books, because then you'll get dumb. But if you use your book as a pillow, you'll get smart."

"Ma!" said Floribeth. "Marisol, getting good grades is a matter of discipline. And God gave you a good brain, so you'll be just fine."

"Lola," said another of the little ones, raising her hand, "If I—ouch! My tongue, my tongue, I bit it, it hurts."

Comforting the child with a hug, Floribeth gave her some water. "Here, drink this, Boogie."

"'Drink this boogie'? Is that what she said? Oh, no, Teacher, please, please don't tell me that's a Filipino thing!"

"Kano, her name is Boogie!"

"Oh."

"Somebody is talking about you," said the Lola to Boogie. "When you bite your tongue, somebody is thinking about you, and you are the subject of their conversation."

"Ma, please."

Just then, the little girl's sister walked in the room. "Boogie, are you okay? We were just talking about how well you did at your dance recital, and how some of the mean moms were jealous."

"Yes, daughter, and you were saying?" said the Lola with a raised eyebrow and slight turn of the head.

"Even a broken clock is right twice a day, Ma."

"Don't sit on a pillow either, children," said the Lola, "or it will slow your recovery from an illness."

"Lola," said a grandchild, trying to slide off the pillow she was sitting on without being noticed, "My friend told me that in the Philippines, there are dwarf monsters."

"Dwarf monsters?" asked the Kano.

"I think she is referring to the *duwende*," said the Teacher.

"Doo Wendy? That sounds familiar. Isn't Doo Wendy the current president of the Philippines?" What a strange name; even sounds a little bit Chinese. Is the Philippine President, Mr. Doo Wendy—is he Chinese?"

"Kano! You're not even pronouncing the name of the dwarf monster right, it's duwende, not Doo Wendy! And, the President's name is Duterte—Rodrigo Duterte. Du-tear-tay. He is the 16th president of the Philippines. And he's not Chinese!"

"Do you know much about him?" asked the Kano.

"A little bit. His full name is Rodrigo 'Rody' Roa Duterte, and—"

"I guess Rody is his nickname. See, I'm getting it; Rody is a short form of Rodrigo," said the Kano proudly.

"No, that's not his nickname."

"Then what is it?"

"Digong."

"Digong? What kind of nickname is that, if his name is Rodrigo?" asked the Kano.

"A perfectly normal one—get your Filipino on! Anyway, he's 71, and is the oldest Filipino to be president. But, you'd never know it—he's got more energy than people half his age."

"Teacher, tell me about these doo-wendy dwarf monsters," said the Kano.

"Duwende are goblin-like mythological creatures. They're mischievous and look like dwarfs. Some believe they lure young children to the forest, causing them to lose their way home. They can provide good, or bad, fortune to humans."

"Oh my," said the Kano.

"In modern day beliefs, duwendes often live in houses, in trees, in underground termite-like mounds or hills, and in rural areas. They can be either good or mischievous, depending on how homeowners treat them," said the Teacher. "They usually come out at 12 noon for an hour and during the night. Filipinos will mutter things like *'tabi-tabi po'* or *'bari-bari apo ma ka ilabas kami apo'* so that the duwendes will excuse them for their disruption. Sometimes, Filipinos leave food on the floor so that the duwende residing in the house, or guarding it, will not be angry with them. The duwende might also take something of yours and laugh at you when you try to find it. They'll give it back when they feel like it, or when you beg them for it."

"Maybe that explains why my car keys are always missing," said the Kano. "My home is infested with doo-wendys. And I thought I was losing my memory, like you, Teacher."

"Kano!"

"Sorry, Teacher."

"Ma, I think you are scaring the children with all that talk of duwendes," said Floribeth.

"Children," said the Lola, "think of the duwende like you think of leprechauns. You're not afraid of leprechauns, are you?"

"No, Lola, but leprechauns don't want to eat you," they said.

"Anak, don't worry," said the Lola. The duwendes don't want to eat you. They just want to take you."

"Aah!" screamed the children.

"But what you must really watch out for are the *aswangs*," said the Lola.

"What are aswangs?" they asked.

"Filipino vampires."

"Aah!" screamed the children

"Aah!" screamed the Kano.

"Kano, an aswang is a monster in Filipino folklore. It's a mix of vampire, ghoul, and witch. Spanish colonists as early as the 16th century called the aswang the most feared mythical creature of the Philippines."

"Why is it called aswang?" asked the Kano.

"Aswang, or asuwang, comes from the Sanskrit word *asura* that means 'demon,'" said the Teacher. "The myth is well known throughout the Philippines, so it's no surprise that the aswang has regional names like tik-tik, wak-wak, sok-sok, and kling-kling."

"Tik-tik, wak-wak, sok-sok, and kling-kling. You're right," said the Kano, "No surprise there."

"Kano, be careful, it sounds like your judging the Filipino's playful nature again when it comes to naming conventions."

"Teacher, I'm sorry, but it's not me, it's my empty stomach being rude. How about an early lunch-lunch?"

"Kano, you've got food on your mind more than Maria. Let's continue our observations."

The Teacher and the Kano walked past some fake plants and trees and stepped into the kitchen. A few people were preparing food, and some others were seated on the kitchen table, talking. Looking toward the sink, the Kano remarked, "That's interesting. Filipino's homes are so clean and tidy, but there is a stack of dishes piled about five feet high in the dish rack. The dishes seem to defy the laws of nature and gravity as to how they are piled on top of each other without falling over."

"Yes, it's an architectural marvel. Some Filipinos think using the dishwasher wastes water. I don't think we'll ever see the Maytag repairman in this home," said the Teacher.

"Oh, over there, on the counter. That's a rice cooker, right? I saw one at Maria's house," said the Kano excitedly.

"Yes, a staple in every Filipino household. Look, Floribeth, the mom, has come into the kitchen to make some rice. She'll use her finger to measure exactly how much water, down to the millimeter, is needed to make the rice just perfect," said the Teacher. "It always amazes me. Whether a Filipino is 4 feet 10 inches or a foot taller, small hands or large, that finger method of measuring how much water to put in the rice cooker always works. Always."

"Now she's struggling to get that giant sack of rice with Middle East writing on it back into the pantry," said the Kano. "How much does it weigh, 100 pounds? Should we help her?"

"Hah, it's not 100 pounds. Not that it's light, because it weighs about 25 pounds. That bag contains Jasmine rice, which has a nice smell to it," said the Teacher, sniffing the air.

"I can see in the pantry giant jugs of soy sauce. Do Filipinos shop at giant discount stores?" asked the Kano.

"No more than anyone else."

"Teacher, I see a flute and clarinet, and some sheet music, next to the kids' backpacks, over there in the corner. Do all Filipino children play musical instruments?"

"Not all, but it's encouraged. Music is an important part of the Filipino culture."

"I guess it must be. At the housewarming party, I heard one of Maria's titas giggling about musical fruits. Are there such fruits in the Philippines?"

"Hah! Yes, such musical fruits are here, too, Kano, but they're not what you think! But yes, music is an important part of the culture. Beauty too. It's not unusual for a Filipina to get involved with beauty pageants."

"I'll be the judge of that, Teacher." The Teacher was stone faced. "Uh, I'll be the judge, you know, the judge of a beauty pageant—but also the judge of your comment. Sort of a double meaning? Get it? Teacher, you're so serious."

"There are some Filipinas that take beauty seriously. Did you know that in the 2001 Miss America Pageant, it was a Filipina who took the title?" asked the Teacher.

"No, I didn't. What's her name?"

"Angela Baraquio. She was the winner in 2001, and the first Asian woman to claim the title."

"Hey, now that you mention Miss America, wasn't it a Filipina who won the Miss Universe a couple of years ago?"

"Yes, Pia Wurtzback. She won the Miss Universe in 2015. She has a Filipino mother and German father—and was raised in the Philippines."

"Was she the first Filipina to win the Miss Universe contest?"

"No, she wasn't. In 1969 Gloria Diaz won. She was the first. Then, four years later, another Filipina won the crown—Margarita Moran. Add Pia, and the Philippines boasts three titles, which puts them in the top-five most-winning countries for the Miss Universe crown," said the Teacher.

"Ouch!" said a voice outside the kitchen. It was Tres, the Lola's grandson. Into the kitchen he walked, looking for some ice. The deep fried pork skin was too tempting to pass up, and in his zeal, he took a bite of his tongue as well.

"Some… body… is talking about you," said the Lola.

"Huh?"

"It never fails," said the Lola. "Just like I said before, when you bite your tongue, it means somebody is talking about you."

"I'm not sure that even a compliment is worth this much pain, Lola. Please, can you get me some ice?"

Turning to the Kano, the Teacher said, "You'll find that the Filipino culture is filled with many interesting expressions and superstitions—they're harmless, really, and I find them quite charming."

"Why are there so many of them?" asked the Kano.

"Well, you've got a melting pot of local and foreign beliefs. There are the original inhabitants of the Philippines—the Negritos, Indonesians, and Malays. And then the newcomers from India, China, and Spain," said the Teacher. "Over time, some of these beliefs just got mixed up together and overlapped and created the superstitions we know today."

Looking upon the kitchen scene again, the Kano saw Floribeth open the pantry door. She reached over cans of sardines to grab some onions, garlic, and tomatoes, and made her way to the stove.

"Onions, garlic, and tomatoes," said the Kano. "What's she going to make?"

"Could be anything. But so long as you sauté it in onions, garlic, and tomatoes, it will taste good," said the Teacher.

"Ma, for the last time, we're not going to have any unexpected visitors over today, okay?" said Floribeth to her mother.

"You sure are. You dropped a spoon," said the Lola.

"What's that all about?" the Kano asked the Teacher.

"The unexpected-visitor thing?"

"Yes."

"Again, it's a superstition. It's said that if you accidently drop a spoon on the ground, an unexpected woman will arrive," said the Teacher.

"What if an unexpected man arrives instead?"

"It means she dropped a fork," smiled the Teacher.

Suddenly, they saw the Lola pushing Ramon, the dad, away from the stove. "Ma, what are you doing?"

"Do you want to lose all your wealth?" she asked. "You don't believe me? Well, it happened to my cousin Toto. One night he was eating his rice and stewed fish eggs by the stove, and the next morning, her bank account was wiped clean."

"That sounds a little....er, well, hard to believe, Ma," said Ramon. "I mean, if you think they are connected."

"It's true. And Toto did other things that were bad for her money," said the Lola.

"Like what?" asked Ramon.

"Well, he tried to sell Amway. Even worse, he owed some money to your titos."

"My titos?" Are we talking about my real titos, or cousins who have been deemed my titos, or someone else's tito who's now my tito, or someone who biologically is my nephew but considered my tito?"

"Yes," said the Lola.

"Yes?"

"Yes, Your Tito Noynoy, Tito Penpen, Tito Dandan, Tito Denden, Tito Lotlot, Tito Nene, Tito Jonjon, Tito Junjun, and Tito Tintin. Oh, and your Tito Tito."

"Am I hearing an echo in here?" asked the Kano.

"Shh!" scolded the Teacher.

"So, Toto owed my titos money. I realize borrowing money is not good, but it's not exactly bad," said the dad.

"Unless you pay back your debt at night."

"What?"

"Paying a debt at night brings bad luck," said the Lola.

"Is that true?" asked the Kano.

"I don't know if it's true or not," said the Teacher. "But if anyone owes me money, I won't stop them from paying me back during the night, believe me."

"What other money expressions or superstitions do Filipinos believe in?" asked the Kano.

"Guess what happens if you borrow money on the first hour of the day, or the first day of the week, or the first day of the month or the first month of the year?" asked the Teacher.

"Uh, should I know this?"

"If you do those things, the belief is that you'll never become rich and will always be hounded by creditors."

"Hmm, so if I borrow on days 2 to 31, I will become rich and never be hounded by creditors. Hey, I'm starting to like these Filipino beliefs," said the Kano.

"Okay, but, don't get too carried away with that one," said the Teacher.

"Do you know any other money superstitions, in case Maria or her relatives say something about money?" asked the Kano.

"I know of a few. Do not spend money on Monday; otherwise, you will go a whole week without money. If you dream of numbers, you will win the lottery. Or, if you see a white butterfly, riches are in store for you."

"I like these," said the Kano. "It's all upside."

"Not all upside," said the Teacher. "It's said that one becomes a poor man if he scrubs the floor at night."

"I can become poor if I scrub the floor at night? That could work. When I'm married to Maria, she won't want me scrubbing the floors past 7 p.m. but would rather, I'm sure, hear me recite the love poems I wrote for her," said the Kano.

"Love poems? Married?"

"I'm just trying to be positive, Teacher. You know, the power of positive thinking," said the Kano.

"You do bring up a very important topic—marriage. Not necessarily yours, Kano—you still need a lot more work. But, it's never too early to prepare," said the Teacher. "For your training tomorrow, I know the perfect place."

"The perfect place? Where would that be, Teacher?" asked the Kano.

"A wedding. But not just any wedding. We're going Filipino style!"

CHAPTER 6
HERE COMES THE BRIDE

"Not again," growled the Kano as he swung widely for the alarm clock, buzzing away at five in the morning.

"*Magandang umaga*," said the Teacher, standing eerily at the Kano's bedside.

"Ma gag Lady ga ga… huh?" said the Kano, trying to wipe the sleep out of his eyes.

"You sound like a baby," said the Teacher. "Lots of ga, ga… you're just missing goo, goo," he laughed.

"Hey, c'mon, what did you say?"

"Magandang umaga. Tagalog for 'good morning.' Here, repeat after me. Mah—ghan—dhaang," said the Teacher.

"Mah—Ghan—Dhaang," repeated the Kano.

"For the next part, it sounds like *you* without the *y*; so 'ou', then, add 'mahga.' Magandang umaga."

"Magandang umaga," said the Kano.

"I feel like Professor Higgins in *My Fair Lady*. I think you've got it, Kano," said the Teacher. "All right, get up and meet me in the kitchen."

The Kano got ready and joined the Teacher, who was drinking a cup of coffee, downstairs in the kitchen.

"Freshly brewed, Kano. Here, have some." As he poured him a strong and rich-smelling cup, he said, "No better way to get your day started, don't you agree?"

Sipping the coffee, the Kano said, "Yes, I do. Teacher, it sounds crazy, because I haven't even gone on a real date with Maria yet, but like I said, I think I really want to marry her. I know she would be the perfect wife for me."

"Kano, I'm not surprised. She's a Filipina, after all!"

"I'm excited about today's training. Are we really going to a wedding?" asked the Kano.

"Yes, but I don't want you to go on an empty stomach, which at this hour of the day, may be the only time that is even possible. Anyway, I thought you might enjoy some *suman* this morning."

"Sue man? Is this one of those he/she things I should know about? Or, is there some kind of legal thing you want to lay on me… like, there's a Filipino lawyer who calls himself Sue Man. Get it? Sue Man? Lawsuit? Teacher? Hello?"

"Kano! Are you losing it? I didn't say 'sue-man,' I said 'suman.' *Mahn.* As in *ahh.* Can you say 'ahh,' like in 'maahn'?"

"Teacher, now you sound like a Filipino-Jamaican dentist!"

"Uy. Suman, I repeat, sue-mahn, is made of a sticky rice cooked in coconut milk and steam wrapped in *buil* or bur palm or corypha leaves. Or, more commonly here in the US, wrapped in banana leaves. It's delicious."

The Kano picked one up from the tray that the Teacher was now holding. With suman in hand, he twisted his hand right and then left, to get a good look at it. He seemed confused. Not sure what to do, he shrugged his shoulders, opened his mouth, and was about to bite into it when the Teacher shouted, "Stop! Stop! Don't eat it yet, it's still in the wrapper!"

"Huh? I thought you said this was delicious. It does look a little tough, though."

"That's because you don't bite into the wrapper! Just think of a banana. You peel the outer wrapper, in this case, the banana leaf, to expose the most wonderful, soft, tasty treat inside," said the Teacher.

"Mmm, this is good, Teacher. Wow, really good!" said the Kano as he eagerly stuffed the suman into his mouth.

"Slow down, slow down. There's more where that came from."

"You made this, Teacher?"

"No, I didn't. I have tried in the past, but failed miserably. Wish I could, because I love them so much. I've used recipe books and watched YouTube videos, but I just can't do it. I think I've been spoiled by Dadak, who makes them so delicious, nothing can compare."

"Dah duck?"

"Yes, Dadak. I made a special trip and got these suman from her."

"Who is she?"

"My wife's cousin. I think. Yes, she's my wife's cousin's mother. Or maybe just a distant cousin. Something like that. A wonderful, gentle soul. She's in her 80s, but she gets up very early before any family party and makes a large tray of delicious suman for us!" said the Teacher.

"Is that how you were introduced to this delicacy?" asked the Kano.

"No; when I first met my wife, she had another cousin, or someone she said was her cousin—I'm not sure if I ever got the story right. But anyway, this cousin person, Goering, made delicious suman too. Hers was the first I had."

Speaking somewhat garbled as his mouth was full of suman, the Kano asked, "Um, okay. What wash this about having to make a special trip?"

"Yes. Well, even though I've failed in trying to make these on my own, I gave it another try this morning, just for you. I even summoned my Filipino cooking spirit to help me make suman: '*Makakatulong sa akin gumawa ang suman*,' I called out, '*makakatulong sa akin gumawa ang suman*,' but still, my cooking skills were just, well, kano."

"So you transported yourself to Dah duk?"

"Yes, I'm not really sure how it happened. I just thought intensely about Dadak's suman, and suddenly, I was at her home in Queens, New York," said the Teacher.

"Then what happened?"

"Well, she was actually in the kitchen, making suman at that very moment! As she was wrapping the suman in banana leaves and putting them on the platter, I was taking some off and putting them in a bag."

"Didn't she notice that her platter was empty, even though she kept putting suman on it? Teacher, she probably thought there was a suman-eating doo-wendy in the house!"

"No, I don't think she suspected any duwendes in the house, although she probably was wondering why it was taking so long to finish. Her platter was about half filled before my arrival. As she continued to make suman and place them on the platter, I was taking every third or fourth one. Poor Dadak! I know she loves to make suman, but I think even she was growing tired, as it took a long time to fill up that platter," said the Teacher.

"Well, you'll have to thank Dah duk for me," said the Kano, "because I really enjoyed these two suman this morning."

"Two?"

"Uh, oh, yes," the Kano said with a nervous laugh. "I guess it was three. Or four. Maybe five? Oh well, who's counting?"

"I am," said the Teacher. "At least I was. I stopped counting at seven."

"Seven? My, how did that happen? But seven is a lucky number. Hey, can that be a Filipino expression?" asked the Kano.

"Can what be a Filipino expression?"

"This. Eating seven or more suman for breakfast brings good luck," said the Kano. "Get it, the luck thing?"

"Do you feel lucky?" asked the Teacher, looking serious.

"Uh, no, not right now," said the Kano nervously. "It looks like you've got your Clint Eastwood Dirty Harry on more than your Filipino spirit, and that makes me nervous. Uh, Filipino spirit-o, or is it espirito? Anyway, hello, Teacher, are you there? Earth calling Teacher? Hello? Pan-de-sal? Hello? Hello?"

"Hah," said the Teacher laughing. "I was just kidding with you."

"Teacher, don't do that! I'm very impressionable."

"I think it's about time we make our way to the wedding." The Teacher smiled, snapped his finger, and out of nowhere the song "Going to the Chapel" filled the kitchen.

"'Going to the Chapel,' nice!" said the Kano, nodding his head to the tune.

"Yes, if you want to marry Maria one day, you should know a thing or two about Filipino weddings and folklore." He turned to the flip chart and added "Filipino Weddings" to the other topics they'd covered.

"What do I need to know?" asked the Kano.

"First, some basics. Repeat after me: kas-a-lan," said the Teacher.

"Kas-a-lan," said the Kano. "What does that mean?"

"It's the Tagalog word for wedding. So, *kasalan* means 'wedding.'"

"Sounds good," said the Kano. "Do I ask Maria, would you like to kasalan with me, baby?"

"Only if you don't want her to marry you," said the Teacher.

"I thought baby was a loved name among Filipinos."

"Yes, but you're no Filipino. At least, not yet—not until I'm done with you," said the Teacher.

"You Kung-Fu guys have no sense of humor."

"Kano, Kung Fu is a Chinese martial art. For the Filipino, the most popular forms of martial arts are Arnis, Eskrima, and Kali. They're similar, and in 2009 President Gloria Arroyo signed a law declaring Arnis as the Philippine National Martial Art and Sport."

"I'll bet she got a kick out of that."

"What I find interesting," said the Teacher, "Is that these fighting systems came about because of the need for self-preservation. Think about it. For ages, the Filipinos had to deal with invaders as well as their own local conflicts. They had to develop battle skills, and today Filipino Martial Arts are considered among the most advanced practical fighting systems in the world. They're used by the US Army, Russian Special forces, and India's Army, Navy, and Police."

"That's really cool."

"Okay, good—now, let's get focused again on the wedding. Filipino wedding customs are said to be influenced by different cultures."

"Not surprising, based on what I've been learning," said the Kano.

"The salutation, greetings, and language of a Filipino wedding come from the courtly Malays and the old Tagalog *principalia*. From the Chinese come the fondness for photography, large receptions and lavish meals, florid bridal adornment, and wedding-cake charms. The pomp, wedding rings, sponsors, coins, veil, doves, and the rice throwing are a Spanish legacy. And the white wedding dress is Anglo-American," said the Teacher.

"It sounds a bit complicated, but I do see how Filipino weddings reflect customs and traditions from other cultures, and how they all come together to make it uniquely Filipino. Check," said the Kano making a check once more in the air with his index finger. "What else should I know?"

"Before there's a wedding, someone's hand must be asked for, right?" asked the Teacher.

"Uh, I guess so. Does that still happen today? I mean, the man going to speak to his girl's father, and asking to marry her? Seems like it's the stuff of old black-and-white movies."

"Trust me, it still happens here in America... but courtship in the Philippines is more traditional than it is in America. In some ways, it's more respectful, and wholesome," said the Teacher.

"When it comes time to ask Maria to marry me, will I have to do it the 'Filipino way'?" asked the Kano.

"No, you don't have to. But you do want to make sure you show respect to her parents."

"Okay, then, tell me a few things. I don't want to mess this up. Uh, I mean when the time comes," said the Kano.

"Sure. Well, here in America we think of the man seeking the permission of the father to marry his daughter," said the Teacher. "In the Philippines, there is a practice called *pamanhikan*, where the parents of the boy call on the parents of the girl to formally ask for her hand in marriage."

"Hmm, I can't see my parents doing that!" said the Kano.

"Don't worry, that's not expected here," said the Teacher. "But don't think of asking Maria to marry you before you speak with her parents."

"Ask parents for permission to marry their daughter. Check," said the Kano.

"Another charming custom is called the *Despedida de Soltera*," said the Teacher. "It is the farewell to the single life and send-off dinner for the daughter before the wedding."

"Kind of like a bachelorette par-tay?" said the Kano enthusiastically.

"Not exactly, thankfully," said the Teacher.

"Is there a wedding season in the Philippines? It's June here in the US, is that right?" asked the Kano.

"Yes, June has traditionally been known as the wedding month, but in recent times, not so much," said the Teacher. "In the Philippines, however, there still is a certain notion of the wedding season."

"What do you mean?" asked the Kano.

"They say December is the marrying-est month among Filipinos," said the Teacher. "Probably true, because just recently, our nephew got married in December, and some years back, my brother-in-law married his bride Donna in Disyembre, back home in the Philippines. As far as the right day of the month, there's a little bit of superstition about that too. An old Filipino rhyme sums it up:

Few marry in August or, on Fridays
Monday for health,
Tuesday for wealth,
Wednesday's the best of all,
Thursday brings crosses and
Friday losses
But Saturday, no luck at all."

"I can't wait to see Maria as my bride," said the Kano. "I'll give her the moon, the stars, the—"

"You're in the OA zone," interrupted the Teacher. "Or maybe the No Way zone. Let's focus. We need to transport ourselves to a wedding celebration where we can observe and you can learn."

"Are we doing the Espiritu thing again? I am seriously down with the Espiritu. Meaning I'm up with it. All right, ready to go," said the Kano, closing his eyes and grabbing onto the teacher's arm with his two hands.

The Teacher closed his eyes and said, "Ang Aking Espiritu Ay Filipino. My spirit is Filipino. Ang Aking Espiritu Ay Filipino. Ang Aking Espiritu Ay Filipino." But unlike before, this time nothing happened. "Kano, join," he said. They both repeated, "Ang Aking Espirtu Ay Filipino, Ang Aking Espirtu Ay Filipino, Ang Aking Espirtu Ay Filipino." Nothing happened.

Opening one eye, the Kano asked, a bit impatiently, "Um, should I let go of your arm now?"

"Now, now, Kano," said the Teacher, "the Espiritu thing doesn't work 100 percent of the time. It's not like we are ghosts or something."

"I only wish."

"Hey, have more faith in your Teacher. I've been doing this for a long time. When the Espiritu chant fails, we turn to the secret weapon," said the Teacher.

"The secret weapon?" asked the Kano.

"Yes," said the Teacher. "The secret weapon." Then with a smile he asked, "Do you Remem-bah?"

"Remem-bah? You mean remember? Remember what?" asked the Kano.

"This!" shouted the Teacher.

Suddenly, the lights dimmed, and the 1970s R&B group Earth, Wind & Fire appeared in the room and started performing "September." The Teacher did what comes naturally to all Filipinos when this song is played at a party—he started line dancing!

"Do you Remem-bah now?" asks the Teacher.

"If you mean 'The 21st night of Septem-bah,' I guess so," said the Kano. "But why are you line dancing?"

"The better question is why are you *not* line dancing?"

"I'm not much of a dancer."

"Well, that's going to change if you want Maria back," said the Teacher, a little out of breath. "Filipinos love to dance. Now, start line dancing while repeating 'Ang Aking Espiritu Ay Filipino' with me, and we should create enough cosmic energy to transport us straight to a Filipino wedding!"

The Kano attempted to mimic the Teacher's line dancing pattern. He wasn't very good, but he was determined. He continued dancing and repeated with the Teacher, "Ang Aking Espiritu Ay Filipino, Ang Aking Espiritu Ay Filipino, Ang Aking Espiritu Ay Filipino!"

In a flash, they found themselves in the middle of a big party that was clearly a wedding reception. The beautiful Filipina bride, radiantly dressed in white with a veil adorned with orange blossoms, was in the middle of the dance floor, and her dress was covered with money.

"We've gone too far," said the Teacher.

"You're telling me," said the Kano. "But what are you telling me, exactly?"

"The powerful combination of 'Do You Remem-bah' line dancing, coupled with our Filipino Espirtu chant, took us right past the wedding and into the reception!"

"As long as we're here, can you tell me why the bride's gown is covered with money? And, hey, look—all the men keep taking turns dancing with her and pinning money on her dress!" said the Kano.

"Yes, it's called the money dance. It's a fun tradition and a way to signal good luck and prosperity for the couple."

The Kano smiled and greedily rubbed his hands together. "The money honey... that's one tradition I want on my wedding day."

"It's been fun crashing the reception, but your instruction today is to learn about the Filipino wedding, not the party. We must go back in time a few hours," said the Teacher.

"How do we do that?"

"Just like we did it before—Ang Aking Espiritu Ay Filipino style. Close your eyes, hold onto my shoulder and think about the wedding ceremony we want to see. Now, repeat after me—'Ang Aking Espiritu Ay Filipino,'" said the Teacher.

The Money Dance

"Ang Aking Espiritu Ay Filipino. Ang Aking Espiritu Ay Filipino. Ang Aking Espiritu Ay Filipino."

In an instant, they were standing at the back of a church.

"Are there any Filipino beliefs or superstitions about weddings?" asked the Kano.

"Yes, there are a few. One is that a bride shouldn't wear pearls on her wedding or else she'll be an unhappy wife and experience many sufferings," said the Teacher.

"No Mikimoto at the bridal shower—check," said the Kano.

They heard some talking in a room adjacent to the vestibule. The door was closed, but they walked right through. The bride they just saw at the reception was now sitting in a small room, talking with the Lola.

"Told you!" said the Kano.

"Told me what?"

"Didn't you see what just happened?" said the Kano. "We walked right through that door, like it wasn't even there—which means we're... we're... ghosts!"

"Uy!" gasped the Teacher. "How many times do I have to tell you, we are not ghosts!"

"Then how did we walk through the door?" asked the Kano.

"You just think there is a door there."

"Huh?" said the Kano. "Of course there's a door, look!"

"Yes, to you, there is a door. To me, there's no door. When my Filipino spirit is on, I am not bound by any physical wall. Since you're with me, neither are you," said the Teacher.

"Am I going to be like you when I get my Filipino spirit on? I'm not so sure about this anymore."

"Shh," said the Teacher. "The bride and the Lola are talking. Let's try to pick up on their conversation."

"Teacher, it's Lola, Mrs. Mendoza's mother," said the Kano excitedly. "You know, Floribeth. But, I don't recognize the bride. Who is she?"

"Her name is Mona Lisa. She is Mrs. Mendoza's sister's daughter—which genealogically makes her a niece to Floribeth."

"And, I shouldn't be amused by her name, Mona Lisa; is that right, Teacher?" asked the Kano.

"Yes, that's right."

"Why did you try on your wedding gown?" asked the Lola to the bride. "Your wedding may be canceled."

"Canceled?" laughed Mona Lisa. "Lola, is this another one of your superstitions? I'm about to walk down the aisle!" she said. "There won't be any cancellations, trust me."

"You haven't walked down yet."

"And you said that I was going to be an old maid," said the bride.

"You did dream of your wedding when you were still single," said the Lola. "When you do that, you become an old maid."

"Oh, you're so funny, Lola. I love the superstitions, but they don't seem to come true very often."

"You can't be too careful," said the Lola. "*Bahala na.*"

"Teacher, bahala na? What does that mean?" asked the Kano.

"Yes, bahala na. It means 'come what may,' or 'whatever will be.' 'Leave it to God,' or 'trust in God'—that sort of sentiment."

"Even you would have to admit, some are pretty funny," the bride continued. "Remember when you told me it would be good luck to marry someone who has a mole on his palms or just below his nostrils?"

"Yes, and you ignored my advice and are marrying this mole-less man of yours," said the Lola.

"What is it with Filipinos and moles?" asked Mona Lisa.

"What do you mean?"

"You also told me not to marry someone who has a mole on his face where tears normally flow!"

"Yes, that's right. Finally, you followed my advice," said the Lola.

"Lola!"

"Did your bridegroom arrive at the church before you? It's bad luck if he came after you."

"Pedro? Don't worry. He was here long before my arrival, Lola."

"Did you warn your parents not to cry during the ceremony?"

"No, uh, why would I say that?"

"Because when the parents cry, it's a bad omen for the newlywed couple," said the Lola. "And for you as well. You can't cry either."

"I can't cry?" asked Mona Lisa.

"No, you will bring bad luck to the marriage."

"Lola!"

"By the way, did you open one of your windows early this morning?"

"No, it was too breezy, and I didn't want any dust blowing in," she said.

"Uy," said the Lola. "You do that so grace will come in. Now, there's no grace."

"Lola! You're making me worried. This is supposed to be the happiest day in my life."

"Oh, it's going to be the happiest day of your life, you say?"

"Of course," said Mona Lisa.

"Then why did you see your husband-to-be last night?"

"Because we're in love, Lola, and can't bear to be a moment away from each other," she giggled.

"Uy," said the Lola. "You know why you ignored my advice? Because you're too OA. Which means you don't listen to your Lola as much as you should. Especially now, when you are vulnerable to bad spirits and goblins."

"Lola, what are you talking about?"

"Because you're so happy and so close to fulfillment, you're open to the spite of bad spirits. By not seeing your asawa-to-be, you trick them and throw them off your trail, so to speak," said the Lola.

"Well, it's too late for that now."

"You could postpone this wedding to the next full moon, and that would keep the bad spirits away."

"In that case, I think it would be a *fool* moon, Lola," she laughed.

"Well, on the bright side, it's not going to thunder today, and that's good because thunder is a bad sign for newlyweds," said the Lola. "There are some rain clouds in the forecast, but that's okay, because rain during a wedding day is a sign of prosperity."

"That's little better, Lola."

As the bride looked at her reflection in the mirror, her Lola tried to tuck bunches of herbs under her veil.

"Lola, what are you doing?" Mona Lisa asked, shielding herself from the herbs.

"It's for the protection of your fertility. You want to have children, don't you?"

"Of course I do, Lola. But not tonight."

"Then let me place some sheaves of grain in your bouquet; that will work too."

"Maybe at my sister's wedding. She wants 12 children."

"Can you lift your gown up a little?" mumbled Lola, who was now on her hands and knees on the floor, holding a sewing needle in between her lips.

"Lola, you're going to ruin your dress! And what you are doing? Sewing? Is my gown ripped? Oh no, my wedding is ruined!"

"It's okay, no worries, your gown is fine. But, since your mother did not sew tiny money bags into the hem of your wedding gown, I'm going to do it now."

"Lola, it's too late to be sewing anything on my gown. The gentlemen can pin money on my gown later, during the money dance. But, you can't sew anything now. Besides, what's it for?"

"It's for good luck, to ensure you will have all the material things you'll need when you're married," said the Lola.

"Oh, Lola, you never seem to run out of these superstitions."

"You might like this one; every woman should love this."

"A superstition I would love? Go on, Lola, what are you talking about?"

"Would you like your new husband Pedro to agree with your every whim?"

"You've got a secret potion?" she asked with a big smile.

"You don't need a potion. Just step on your groom's foot while walking towards the altar."

Laughing, she said, "I don't think I'll step on my bridegroom's foot."

"Okay, fine, don't step on his foot. But just so you know, you can still gain some dominance by being the first to stand up right after the ceremony—just be sure to lean on your husband's shoulder. Or, another way is to fold your veil and place it underneath the wedding bed."

"Lola, we love each other. Our marriage is going to be equal, 50-50."

"As it should be… I'm just concerned that he doesn't have the mole."

"Lola, I love you," said Mona Lisa as she gave her a big hug.

The Teacher and the Kano walked back through the door and sat in a pew in the back of the church. The wedding was about to get underway.

"The day of the wedding is called 'The Bride's Day,'" said the Teacher.

"How different is it from an American wedding?" asked the Kano.

"If you mean from an American Catholic wedding, not so different. But, there are some things about it that make it uniquely Filipino," said the Teacher.

"Really, like what?"

"There is the tradition of the principal sponsors called the *padrino* and *madrina*, or the *ninong* and *ninang*," said the Teacher.

"Knee nong? Sponsors? I'm not sure I understand," said the Kano.

"The principal sponsors' original function was to stand as witnesses to the marriage. In the Philippines, marriage is an alliance between two households, a form of social security," said the Teacher. "Over time, the role of the witnesses evolved into sponsors, the responsible godfather and godmother of a couple at marriage. That's what ninong and ninang mean—the 'godfather' and 'godmother.'"

"Was *The Godfather* starring Marlon Brando called *The Ninong* starring Marlon Brando when the movie played in the Philippines? Uh, by the look on your face Teacher, I'll just withdraw that question."

"The ninong and the ninang are supposed to be the second parents or counselors for the couple," said the Teacher. "They say the more the merrier—so you can imagine, some weddings can be very merry! But, to be safe, most parishes set a maximum of four to six principal sponsors for the wedding."

"Principal sponsors, check," said the Kano.

"There are some other sponsors as well," said the Teacher.

"More?"

"Yes, there are the veil, cord, and candle sponsors," said the Teacher.

"This is getting complex!"

"Oh, at first it may seem that way, but it all fits together beautifully," said the Teacher. "Let's start with the veil sponsors. They drape a veil over the couple to cover the bride's head and the groom's shoulder."

"Okay, tell me the superstition with this one," said the Kano.

"No superstition. It's to signify that the bride's head should rise no higher than her husband's shoulder."

"You mean, like, he's in charge? Whoa, I'm likin' this custom," said the Kano.

"Hold on, it's not like that. Remember, the Philippines remain a culture steeped in tradition. That doesn't mean a husband is superior to his wife, but they do have different roles in family life," said the Teacher. "As Catholics, we believe that a husband should love his wife as Christ loves the church, and the wife should obey her husband as the head of the family."

"Obey? Oh yay," said the Kano.

"You're getting caught up in semantics. It's all about family life. That's why I'm so drawn to the Filipino culture, and think the Filipina makes such a wonderful wife. She puts her family first. Believe me, your Filipina will not be kowtowing to your every demand," said the Teacher.

"What do the candle sponsors do?"

"The candle sponsors light the two candles beside the bride and groom to invoke the light of Christ in their married life," said the Teacher.

"And the cord?"

"After the veil has been placed," said the Teacher, "the cord sponsors lay a cord, or a ribbon or a string of flowerets in the form of a figure eight and—"

"Figure eight?" asked the Kano.

"Yes, a figure eight is the mathematical sign of infinity, and a symbol of unending devotion. The cord is placed over the shoulders of the bride and groom."

"I like that—unending devotion," said the Kano.

"Yes, unending devotion that goes both ways," said the Teacher.

"Of course."

"The cord can also be thought of as a yoke, to remind the couple of the burdens of matrimony they'll both carry."

"Burdens?" said the Kano. "What just happened to unending devotion?"

"Oh, I forgot, there's one more sponsor," said the Teacher.

"Another sponsor?"

"Yes, the coin sponsor. The coins, or *arras*, are supposed to symbolize the groom's dowry to the bride," said the Teacher.

"Dowry? You mean money? Teacher, I'm young... you know, I'm still just establishing myself. Will Maria expect a dowry from me?"

"Kano, this isn't about you, it's about learning to appreciate the diverse and beautiful traditions of the Filipino wedding."

"Yes, it is. Veil, candle, cord, and coins sponsors; check," said the Kano.

"There are a few other wedding superstitions I'm aware of that you might find interesting," said the Teacher.

"Sure, shoot."

"The bride isn't supposed to try on her wedding dress before the wedding."

"Huh, that sounds risky," said the Kano.

"Doing so is supposed to bring bad luck. To get around it, the bride should only try on the slip or the lining."

"So much for the 'Say Yes to the Dress' show," said the Kano. "They'll need a new rhyme. Maybe 'I'm hip with the slip' or 'Time to go dining, I'm good with the lining.'"

"Are you this nonsensical around Maria?" asked the Teacher.

"She cares about me for who I am, not as the world sees me."

"Oh, brother," sighed the Teacher. "Anyway, some other superstitions for the bride, and I suppose the groom too, are to stay away from sharp knives, steep stairs, and long journeys as the wedding day approaches."

"Let me guess why. Hmm, so it doesn't bring bad luck?" asked the Kano.

"And the bride should never marry in the same year as her sister... the same for the bridegroom. He shouldn't marry the same year as his brother," said the Teacher. "It's called *sukob sa taon*, meaning no siblings should marry in the same year."

"I'm sure the bride's father likes that one!" said the Kano. "Sukob sa taon—bring it on! Oh, I forgot to ask you: When we were at the reception, the bride was wearing orange blossoms in her veil. It looked beautiful and I've never seen that before," said the Kano.

"Yes, it is beautiful, and there's a meaning behind it. The orange tree is an evergreen, and a symbol of the bridal pair's love for each other," said the Teacher. "Also, I've heard that because the orange tree bears blossoms and fruits at the same time, the ancients took this to signify a double-strength hope for fertility."

"Ancient wisdom," said the Kano.

"You know, now that we're talking oranges, and this is completely off topic, but you might find it interesting—I remember when my wife's family was supporting Filipino businessman and former senator Manny Villar, when he was running for the President of the Philippines," said the Teacher.

"Is Manny a popular name… for mans… I mean men… in the Philippines? Boxers, senators…," joked the Kano.

"Maybe. Anyway, I remember we were at a family party, and when it came time for the group picture—you know, the one where 28½ smiling Filipinos try to fit on a small couch together, shouting 'Picture! Picture!'—we were all holding oranges, to show our support for the senator," said the Teacher.

"Why oranges?"

"Villar's campaign color was orange," said the Teacher.

"Did he win?" asked the Kano.

"He represented himself and the Nacionalista Party well, but didn't win. His campaign slogan was *Sipag at Tyaga*, or *Hard Work and Patience*. Who could argue with that? The Senator himself grew up poor and, through grit and determination became one of the country's richest men. He's a genuine rags-to-riches Horatio Alger story. And, I know from first-hand accounts, he's a good family man and readily shares his blessings with others. Politics is a rough-and-tumble sport in the US, but in the Philippines, it's even tougher—a blood sport, they say."

No couch is too small for picture-picture & wacky-wacky

"Blood orange sport," said the Kano.

"Yes, blood orange."

The Teacher and the Kano relaxed and watched the beautiful Filipino wedding unfold before their eyes. When it was over, the Teacher turned to the Kano. "I think it's time for us to leave. Ready to go?"

"What about the reception? I've got my dancing shoes on, Teacher!"

"I thought you didn't like to dance. Anyway, the point of this was to teach you some things about the Filipino wedding, and now that the ceremony is over, it's time for us to go."

"Uh, sure, okay," said the Kano, disappointed. "But, how are we going to get out of here?"

"Do you Remem-bah?" asked the Teacher.

"Remem-bah? I'd rather forget," said the Kano.

They arrived back at the Kano's place and sat down at the kitchen table.

"How did you do it?" asked the Kano.

"Do what? My wedding? My marriage?" asked the Teacher.

"Yes, how did you go about it? You know, ask your asawa to marry you," said the Kano.

"Oh, yes. Well, I wanted to be respectful to my wife's parents," said the Teacher. "So, because of some language constraints, I asked if she would let her parents know I'd be stopping by on a specific day and time to say hello."

"Wasn't she suspicious?" asked the Kano.

"Yes, she knew what I was up to, but I remained close-mouthed."

"How did it go? I mean, of course, it went well, you married her, but tell me how it went." asked the Kano.

"Like I said, I wanted to be respectful, so my plan was to ask for her hand, in Tagalog, the native tongue of her parents," said the Teacher.

"How did you do that?"

"I asked my future sister-in-law, Marites, to help with the translation. I put it on an index card, and memorized as much as I could," said the Teacher.

"And…?"

"I drove into New York City where they lived. When I knocked on the apartment door, it was opened by two of their grandchildren, Christine and Cathy. I was so happy they were visiting because children are always a great distraction and I thought would help me ease into the conversation," said the Teacher.

"So long as they are not too distracting, especially when you're there to ask for their daughter's hand in marriage," said the Kano.

"Yes, well, they weren't distracting at all. In fact, their lola shooed them away to the bedroom immediately upon my arrival!"

"Oh, no."

"Yes, so much for small talk. Her mother quickly pulled a kitchen chair into the small living room area for me, and then she and my wife's father sat on the couch… directly across from me, just a few feet away, and well, just smiled in that beautiful, Filipino way and looked at me," said the Teacher.

"They just smiled and looked at you? What were you thinking?"

"This is it!" said the Teacher. "No *babalik ako* for me. Not that I would have wanted that anyway—the time was now."

"Showtime!"

"I guess it was."

"So, they gave you their blessing. Whew! Then, when it was time for you to get married, was the wedding Filipino style?" asked the Kano.

"If you mean did we have principal sponsors and veil, candle, cord, and coin sponsors, yes, we did," said the Teacher.

"That's really cool."

"As I fell in love with the woman who would be my wife, I fell in love with her culture, the culture of the Philippines. Embracing and celebrating some Filipino wedding traditions seemed perfectly natural to me," said the Teacher.

"I'm going to follow in your footsteps, Teacher. Well, sort of. Ghosts don't really have footprints."

"Teacher, why did it become pitch black? And I don't hear the ocean. We're not at the beach? Isn't this going to be one of our lumpia moments? Uh, Teacher, I'm serious; I can't see anything—except your eyes! I can only see your eyes! Teacher, are you trying to scare me? Because if you are, it's working!"

"Kano! Get hold of yourself."

"Uh, okay, if you want to have a conversation in the dark, fine; that's just fine, Teacher. Yup, no problem. I'm just fine," said the Kano, his voice a bit shaky. "But why do you want to have a conversation in the dark, anyway?"

"The dark? Do you call this the dark?" asked the Teacher, as he snapped his fingers expectantly, waiting for something to happen. But nothing happened.

"Teacher?"

"Yes, Kano?"

"Uh, since it's still pitch black, can you focus some of your thought vibrations on a light switch, or is there anything you might remember about getting out of a situation like this?"

"Did you say… 'remem-bah'?"

Smiling, the Kano replied, "Yes, yes, I did say 'remem-bah.'"

"Hit it," the Teacher cried out. Suddenly, the space filled with disco ball lighting and the sound of "September." "Time to get your line dancing on, Kano! Tell me what you learned."

The Kano attempted to follow the Teacher's moves. "Well, I learned a lot about Filipino weddings, and principal sponsors and the chain and veil—er, I mean the cord and veil traditions," said the Kano, as he rocked forward and back to the music. "Love the money dance. I can see my beautiful bride Maria, orange blossoms in her veil, her wedding gown pinned with tens and twenties. What about fifties? Will anyone pin $50 bills on my bride, Teacher? And, in case people are short on cash, is it okay to take checks? Checks can be pinned on just as easily, Teacher. Don't you think? There's even a way to take credit cards nowadays through your iPhone. Can we take cash, checks, and credit cards for the money dance? It's the age of technology, you know."

"Kano! Since you think you're going to marry Maria one day, I'd suggest you take this topic more seriously," said the Teacher as he did a cross cha to the Kano's cha basic.

"Sorry Teacher, I got carried away," he said, in the middle of a jazz square. "I really do like the traditions—the Despedida de Soltera for the soon-to-be bride, the wedding superstitions, and how the boy's whole family asks the girl's parents for her hand."

Shuffling to the right, the Teacher replied, "They say when you marry a Filipina, you marry her whole family."

"I'm glad Maria has a big family, Teacher, because that sounds good to me!" said the Kano as he caught his breath and went into a side shuffle.

"I not only liked what you said, Kano, I liked the way you said it. You're ready for another lumpia shanghai, to acknowledge your continuing progress—here. There is something more though, something more I'd like to see from you right now."

"Something more?" asked the Kano excitedly. He remembered what the Teacher had said after the first day of training... that to win Maria's heart, he'd need more than just knowledge. He'd need to know *something more*. "Teacher, please don't hesitate—tell me right now what you want to see. I'm ready."

"A mambo."

"A mambo? You want to see a mambo? That's the 'something more' that will win Maria's heart?"

"Well, it's not the *something*-something more I want to see from you, but since you're starting to get the hang of this line dancing thing, believe me, it won't hurt."

CHAPTER 7
SUPERDUPER-STITIONS

"Aah!" yelled the Kano, slamming the alarm clock at 5 a.m. as he abruptly sat up in bed.

"Good morning, Kano," said the Teacher.

"I'm never going to get used to you just showing up like this."

"When your brain isn't thinking of Maria all the time, and you're not so worried about the relationship, I won't show up," said the Teacher.

"You won't?" asked the Kano, seemingly disappointed.

"No; you won't need me. You'll have finished your training. You will have taken the lumpia shanghai from my hand… and you will have *mano-po'd*."

Frustrated, the Kano said, "Can you please tell me what this lumpia taking–mano pak-ee-yoh thing is all about?"

"In good time, Kano, in good time," said the Teacher. "Another day is upon us. Meet me in the kitchen after you get yourself together."

"Teacher, I'm so tired. How about we take today off and start fresh tomorrow?"

"I'll be waiting for you downstairs."

In about half an hour, the Kano was in the kitchen, looking surprisingly awake and motivated. "Teacher, pour me a cup of Joe, I'm ready to go."

The Teacher's back was to him, as he was writing something on the flip chart.

"What are you… are you writing 'Birthday'? 'Birthday Party'?" asked the Kano excitedly. "I love birthday parties, especially when they're for me!"

Turning around to face him, the Teacher replied, "Yes, 'Birthday Party.' No, not for you. And, this is not just any birthday party. It's a child's first birthday. That means there will be a huge celebration."

"Whose birthday? Where? Will we be celebrating with food, Teacher?"

"Is the sky blue, Kano?"

"Uh, sometimes it's blue… but it can also be a pale blue… and other times it looks kind of white. Why are you asking me about the sky, Teacher?"

"Kano, to ask if Filipinos celebrate with food is like asking whether the sky is blue."

"Huh?"

"Uy, yes, there will be food, lots of it. Whose birthday? you asked. And where? For today's instruction, we are going to rejoin the Mendoza family at their home, where they are hosting a birthday party for their niece, Rhea, who is one year old."

"I really do love birthdays," said the Kano, "especially the birthday cake. Why is the first birthday such a big celebration?"

Smiling, they both said together, "For good luck!"

"How are we getting there, Teacher? Espiritu? Or, Remem-bah Septem-bah?"

"We're going Espiritu, as you say. Ang Aking Espirtu Ay Filipino," said the Teacher.

"Uh, yes, Ang Aking Espiritu Ay Filipino," the Kano joined in. "Ang Aking Espiritu Ay Filipino."

Poof! In an instant, they were transported back to the Mendoza home.

"Ma, can you put the flyswatter underneath the sink and wipe down our vinyl-covered kitchen table?" asked Floribeth as she walked into the kitchen from the family room. "Oh, and can you take the aluminum foil covering off the stove and put it away? Our guests will be here soon."

Her mother, the Lola, adorned with jewelry and wearing a beautiful dress, said "Okay, and then I'll dust the piano that nobody plays and the useless trinkets that nobody sees."

"You said this was going to be a huge celebration, Teacher, but it's already past noon, and nobody is here," said the Kano.

"Yes, so?" asked the Teacher.

"So, nobody is here," said the Kano.

"I'm not following you."

"It's past noon!" shouted the Kano. "The party starts at noon, and nobody is here."

"Oh, now I get it. You think the party is supposed to start at noon?" asked the Teacher.

"Yes, that's the start time on the invitation that you showed to me before."

"Clearly, you're not familiar with Filipino time," said the Teacher.

"Is that like Miller time?" said the Kano thirstfully.

"No, that would be more like San Miguel time. Filipino time is... I mean, basically, it means being late," said the Teacher.

"Fashionably late?"

"That's a good way to look at it. Filipinos are very fashionable, like Josie Natori, the famous Filipino fashion designer, and sometimes they can be fashionably late; I like that," said the Teacher.

"Seriously, tell me about this late thing."

"Well, I don't mean everybody is always late for things, but there's a sentiment among Filipinos, almost an expectation, that being late to a party or event is sort of expected or at least understood," said the Teacher.

"Why is that?"

"I'm not exactly certain. I've heard that the term was coined to mean Filipino *Indios* time. Like a lot of things in the Philippines, it can be traced back to the Spanish colonization period," said the Teacher.

"Filipino Indians?" asked the Kano. "Like American Indians? I've never heard that before."

"Right, because you wouldn't have heard that before!" said the Teacher, a little annoyed. "I said Indios, meaning 'second citizen.' During the years of colonization, when there were parties or other social gatherings, there was a need to distinguish between the upper class señores' and señoritas' time and the so-called second citizens' time."

"Are you saying that the Filipinos were forced to come late?" asked the Kano.

"Yes. The Spaniards required them to come later, after the conquistadores and mestizos had all been properly greeted by the host and seated. The food may have already been served, and the Filipinos would save face by saying they had already eaten," said the Teacher.

"Doesn't sound very nice, especially for such kind, warm people," said the Kano, a little sad.

"It was the times. And over time, this 'time thing' became tradition and culture. Let's face it, 300 years of Spanish colonization can do that to a people!"

"I guess."

"But now, Filipinos are playful with this idea of a vague timeline; they kind of laugh about it. And I think it's a reflection of their spirit—the history of the Filipino is overcoming one adversity after another. On the one hand there's bahala na, and on the other there's self-determination," said the Teacher.

"Bahala na?" asked the Kano. "Wait, wait, don't tell me, because you already told me about this bahala nana thing—uh-uh. Sorry, Teacher, please tell me again; I'm drawing a blank."

"Bahala na doesn't really have a direct translation in English, Kano, but again, it basically means 'come what may' or 'leave it to God'; or, you could think of the Spanish phrase *'que sera sera*,'" said the Teacher.

"'Que sera sera.' That reminds me of my great-grandmother. She liked to listen to Englebert Humperdinck's rendition of the song," said the Kano.

"Believe it or not, my brother-in-law is named after Englebert Humperdinck."

"Your brother-in-law's name is Englebert Humperdinck?" asked the confused Kano. "That doesn't sound Filipino."

"Yes, his name is Gilbert."

"Gilbert?" asked the puzzled Kano.

"Sure. Eng-gil-bert. Gil-bert. Get it?"

"I'm starting too."

"But we call him Ibet."

"So much for getting it," said the Kano.

"Anyway, regarding bahala na, just know that Filipinos may say this when they're unclear about the future, but accepting of what the outcome might be. For many, it's about submitting humbly to God's will, and trusting in His greater power."

"I see. And you said something about self-determination?" said the Kano. "What do you mean?"

"Yes, I think a good example is this Filipino time thing. On the one hand, there's the bahala-na-ness to it. But, some years back, there was actually an official government effort to address it," said the Teacher.

"What do you mean?"

"In 2011, the Philippine Department of Science and Technology, or DOST, launched a public awareness campaign called 'Juan Time' and—"

"Juan time?" interrupted the Kano.

"It was a word play on *one time*, and the campaign promoted time-consciousness among Filipinos. The goal was to encourage nationwide use of the Philippine Standard Time or PST, the country's official time," said the Teacher.

"So they took the bull by the horns, so to speak," said the Kano.

"Maybe more like taking the carabao by the horns," said the Teacher.

The Mendoza family continued to prepare for their guests. Floribeth was sweeping the kitchen floor.

"Whoa, what is that?" asked the Kano.

"What is what?" asked the Teacher.

"The mom, Mrs. Mendoza, what is she sweeping with?" asked the Kano. "It looks like something Broom Hilda would use."

"Now, now," said the Teacher, "remember your goal here."

"Sorry. I'm not being disrespectful; it's just that, that broom... it looks like—"

"It's called a *walis tambo*," interrupted the Teacher, "it's actually a very good sweeper. And not nearly long enough for Broom Hilda."

"Why such a funny name, if I can ask that?"

"Sure. Well, the word *walis* means 'broom,' and tambo is the name of a reed. Walis is a soft broom, made from the reeds. My sister-in-law Sahlee always seems to be walis-tambo-ing around the house when guests are visiting. She always sweeps with a big, warm smile, so it must be much better than a Swiffer!" said the Teacher.

"Maybe I'll get one for Maria," said the Kano.

"Yes, and why don't you give her a toaster too, Mr. Romance," said the Teacher. "By the way, there's another broom, called the *walis ting-ting* that is for outdoor sweeping. It's made from the stiff ribs of palm leaves. It looks a little odd because there's no handle—it's just tied up on one end. Now that I think of it, I should get one for our outdoor patio; it really works well."

A little after 1:00 p.m., the guests started arriving. By three o'clock, the house was packed. A mountain of shoes, sneakers, and high heels had accumulated in the foyer.

"Whoa," said the Kano. "That's a lot of shoes!"

"Always a sign of a successful party. As you've learned, Filipinos take their shoes off when entering a home," said the Teacher.

"I see Mrs. Mendoza, uh, Floribeth, greeting her guests with kisses on the cheek; and is she speaking Spanish? Teacher, it sounds like she's saying *como esta*, you know, 'How are you?'" said the Kano.

"Not como esta but *kumusta*," said the Teacher. "She's saying 'kumusta.' And, yes, it means 'How are you?' in Tagalog."

"Coo-moo-sta," repeated the Kano.

"Yes, kumusta. And, did you hear her say '*kain na*'?" asked the Teacher. "She's inviting them to eat."

"I remember hearing that said at Maria's party," said the Kano. "Uh, why is the Lola smelling the children?"

"It's a sniff kiss. Common among lolas and titas," said the Teacher. "They come close like they are going to kiss you and at the same time, they sort of sniff and inhale."

"Dingdong, Bing-bing and Bong-bong—kumusta?" said Floribeth. "You look hungry, eat!"

"Uh, I don't want to seem rude, but what's with the doorbell-sounding names?" asked the Kano.

"I'm not really sure," said the Teacher. "Again, a lot of things are going on with Filipino names that I gave up trying to understand a long time ago. Like, a nickname that suits someone when they're 2, like Honey Boy, sticks with them, even when they're a 50-year-old father and banker."

"Honey Boy, that's kind of funny," said the Kano. "Uh, I mean, you know, for a grown man."

"Yes, but, I rather like it. There's a genuine-ness to it," said the Teacher. "And sometimes a name seems fairly customary, like our niece Sofe. But her full, given name is Dearsofe. And she is a dear, so it fits perfectly. In any event, I think it all shows that Filipinos are confident and self-assured and have a great penchant for fun."

"I guess you're right."

"Just look at the past president of the Philippines, Benigno Aquino. He's called Noynoy!" said the Teacher. "And as an aside, two of his sisters are called Pinky and Ballsy, and no one seems to notice!"

"How was it for you, when you first met your wife's family?" asked the Kano.

"You mean their names?" said the Teacher.

"Yes."

"Nothing too unusual, I guess," said the Teacher. "I didn't know it at the time, but as you've learned, Filipino names can be a combination of their first, and first middle name, or their third middle name and a portion of their second middle name or their mother's maiden name and—"

"Yes, yes, I've heard," said the Kano.

"So, I was having a little trouble at first remembering the names of two of my future brothers-in-law. Not the name itself, so much, but which name was for whom," said the Teacher.

"Huh?"

"One of my brothers-in-law is named Babut, and the other Bobot. Babut and Bobot. Once, I was greeting them both at the same time, and I called Babut Bobot and Bobot Babut. Realizing my mistake, I tried to pivot quickly in reverse to get it right," said the Teacher. "It sounded like babubobubat... you know, when you move your finger over your lips to make a b-b-b-b-b sound?"

"Yes," said the Kano.

"Well, that's what I sounded like. A blathering fool! Fortunately, my future brothers-in-law just smiled politely at my gaff," said the Teacher.

Looking past the kitchen and into the formal living room, the Kano noticed all the multicolored streamers hung across the ceiling, party favors, prizes for games, lots of balloons, and a table full of presents for the celebrant. "Wow, this is really amazing... and completely color-coordinated. And, all of the party favors are meticulously placed next to each other, 3½ centimeters apart, as if they were in a precise military formation."

"Yes, very typical. A lot of work goes into planning any Filipino party, especially giveaways for a first birthday."

"And like you said, there's lots of food! Looks like the dining room table is filled with about 20 delicious dishes, all in aluminum trays."

"Yes, there's a lot. Again, the Filipino way is to ensure that no one goes hungry. Some of the dishes you see today are *pancit*, a noodle dish with carrots and cabbage and chicken. It's especially appropriate for a birthday, as the pancit noodle, being long, is encouragement for the celebrant to have a long life. There's also spaghetti, Filipino style, with sliced hot dogs, and puto, which you might remember is steamed rice cake, and amazingly delicious."

"You had me at pancit," said the Kano.

"There's ukoy, a vegetable and shrimp fritter; pancit molo, which is a Filipino pork dumping soup; and escabeche, a sweet and sour fish recipe. Oh, and I see a baked ham. I'm sure it's good, but my sister-in-law Malou owns the baked ham—hers is the best."

"Not something you want to skip, right, Teacher? Skip the ham? Get it?"

"Huh?"

"Skip to Malou, my darling. You've never heard that song before? C'mon, that one's old enough for you to know."

"Kano! It's Skip to My Lou—My Lou! Not Malou! The Lou part of the title comes from the Scottish word for love—*lou*. Skip to My Lou was a popular dance in the 1840s."

"Oh, uh, isn't that interesting."

"And I'm sure you've noticed the interesting tray of skewers made with hotdog and marshmallow. It's not so common to serve those here in the US; but as you can see, it's playful for a kid's party, and they love them."

"Hot dog and marshmallow skewers?" said the Kano to himself, but he was preoccupied with something else on the table. "Yes, and, uh, ah, something, something else is on the, it's… Teacher, is that a… a… pig? On the table? Sitting right there, on top of the dining room table? Staring at me?"

"Yes, it's a pig, but we call it *lechon*."

"Luncheon?" asked the Kano. "You call a pig a luncheon? I guess that makes sense, if you eat it after breakfast and before dinner."

"Kano, not luncheon, lechon. Lechon is a Spanish word that means a roasted, suckling pig. As you can see, it's the whole pig. Lechon is a national dish of the Philippines, and it's delicious."

"Uh, sorry; didn't mean to sound so alarmed."

"No worries. It's not every day that a kano sits down at the table with a fully roasted pig staring at him. Do you see that bottle next to it? That's Mang Tomas, a sauce for the pork."

"Mang Toe Mass? That doesn't sound too appetizing Teacher. Does it have something to do with Filipinos being Catholic? You know, Mass? Or perhaps a toe condition you need to see a podiatrist about?"

"Kano! Tomas—sounds like toh-mahss—not Toe Mass! Mang Tomas is a condiment, like ketchup. But, you won't find any tomatoes in it. It's made with crushed pork liver, water, sugar, vinegar, breadcrumbs, and spices; it's sweet, thick, and tangy."

"Why is it called Mang Tomas?"

"The name comes from its inventor, Tomas de los Reyes. Back in the 1950s he started selling pork meat outside his house in Quezon City, in the Philippines, and later ventured into selling pre-roasted pork, a convenience his customers loved. This led to starting his own piggery, creating his legendary liver sauce and opening a restaurant. President Magsaysay, the country's 7th President, was one of the eatery's most distinguished guests, and the famed roasted pig even made an appearance at several Malacañang Palace banquets, which is the official residence of the President."

"Teacher, I don't recall seeing a roasted piggy at Maria's housewarming party. Is it served only at birthday parties?"

"No, it can be served anytime, but often you'll find it at special occasions like today."

"Any other desserts, beside the cake?" asked the Kano.

"*Halo-halo.*"

"Uh, and hallow to you too, Teacher. Why are you saying hello to me now? We've been together for hours."

"Kano, I'm pointing out the halo-halo on the dessert table. Hmm, it's so refreshing and delicious, especially on a hot day."

"What is it exactly?"

"It's a colorful mixture of shaved ice, evaporated milk, and a variety of ingredients like sugar palm fruit, sweetened plantains, jackfruit, tapioca, sweet potato, coconut, and sweet beans. It's often topped with *ube* ice cream or *leche* flan."

"Ooh-beh? Lechay flan?" asked the Kano.

"Yes, ube is a purple yam, and is made into ice cream, as well as lots of other sweet treats. It's delicious."

"Ooh beh-beh," said the Kano. "And the lechay flan?"

"It's a rich, steamed custard with a syrupy caramel. Leche is Spanish for milk, and the dessert is made with evaporated milk, sweetened condensed milk, and egg yolks. It's a staple in celebratory feasts. I became a fan of flan, so to speak, when I first had my brother-in-law Rey's flan. Amazingly delicious, but there was a downside."

"A downside? To being a flan fan?"

"Yes, his is so good, nothing else compares!"

"Speaking of celebratory feasts, when will they sing Happy Birthday to the baby? I mean, I guess Filipinos sing Happy Birthday, don't they, Teacher?"

"Of course! What kind of question is that?"

"Yes, er, I know they sing Happy Birthday, who doesn't? But is it sung in English or Filipino?"

"Ahh, yes, it's sung in English, here, for sure. The Tagalog translation for Happy Birthday is *maligayang kaarawan*.

"I don't think I'll even try to pronounce that one," said the Kano.

Clearing his throat, the Teacher started to sing the Happy Birthday song, Filipino style:

"Maligayang bati,

Maligayang bati,

Maligayang, maligayang,

Maligayang bati."

"The tune sounds exactly like Happy Birthday," said the Kano, "it's just that I can't understand any of it. Not that you were mumbling, Teacher, although, to be honest, some voice lessons wouldn't hurt."

"Kano!"

"Hey, talking about singing Happy Birthday, it's time to sing it for the celebrant. Look, everyone's gathering around the cake. And they're so excited. The candle's been lit and the baby, who now is wearing a birthday hat, is being held by the mom in front of the cake. How cute. I should move over to make room for others and—"

"Kano, you don't need to move over."

"I don't need to move over to make room? Because I'm not taking up space? Is that what you're implying, Teacher? I'm not taking up space? Which means that I'm really a gho—"

"No, you're not—you're not a ghost! It's just that everyone has finished singing, blown out the candles and left the room with their pieces of spongy birthday cake. Kano, are you listening to me? Hello? Did you disappear into Never-Never Land?"

"Uh, sorry, I was just thinking of Maria. Anyway, is that it? The party's over?"

"A Filipino party never seems to end. I mean, it does, eventually, but this one certainly isn't ending anytime soon." Pointing to the window, the Teacher said, "Look outside— the kids have gathered to play *pabitin*."

The Teacher and the Kano walk through the kitchen and out the sliding glass doors to the deck, to have a better view of the children playing in the yard. "They're very excited," said the Kano. "What did you say they are playing?"

"Pabitin. It's something you'll see in the Philippines, not so much in the US, but lucky for you the Mendozas are having some traditional fun at this party. It's a bonus for your training. Anyway, pabitin is played at birthday parties or town fiestas. As you can see, there's a lattice of bamboo sticks, called a *balag*, that's suspended in the air. And do you see those small plastic bags tied to the lattice? They're filled with small toys, coins, snacks, and treats. The tito has suspended the lattice so he can lower and raise it quickly. When the balag, or bamboo stick lattice, is lowered up and down, the children jump at it and try to grab a prize bag."

One of the titos who had taken charge of the game began lowering and raising the balag, and the children were screaming, jumping, and laughing... and some were crying when they couldn't get their hands on the prized bag. "Teacher, is this the Filipino version of a piñata?"

"There's another game called *pukpok palayok* that's more similar to a piñata, and I'll tell you about that in a minute. By the way, pabitin is sometimes called *paagaw*, meaning 'anything for grabs.'"

"Well, that makes sense, for sure."

"Interestingly, the game is rooted in Catholicism. It's played during Santa Cruz de Mayo, which is a commemoration of the search for Christ's cross by Saint Helen and her son, Constantine the Great."

"That is interesting. I'm really liking all this history of the Philippines. I can't wait to impress Maria."

"Kano, the point of your training isn't to impress Maria, it's... well, you'll want to do something more than just try to impress her."

"Huh? 'Something more' again? You mean, after I go through all this lumpia shanghai-ing, I'm not going to impress Maria? How am I going to win her heart? That's the point of all this, isn't it, Teacher?"

"Kano, what did I tell you when I first appeared?"

"Uh, good morning? Hello? Teacher, sorry, I don't remember. It was five o'clock in the morning—I was half-asleep!"

"Pagbabagong-anyo. Ring a bell? Transformation? You need to be transformed in order to win Maria's heart. Hello?"

"Yes, yes, of course. Paga-ga-gong show something or other. Yes, sorry, that's right; I'm not going to impress Maria. Nope. No impressing. Not today." After a few moments of looking down and confused, the Kano, with surprising humility, asked, "But Teacher, then how am I going to win Maria's heart if I can't impress her? That I know all about her culture. That I've changed."

"Kano," said the Teacher gently, "Maria is not going to care if you know a lot about Filipinos and their ways, but she does want to know that you care—about her, her heritage, her customs, and her family. That's what your training is all about—because the more you learn about Filipinos and their culture, believe me, the more you will love Filipinos and their culture."

"Thank you, Teacher," said the Kano as he observed all the children laughing and running from the balag, prize bags in hand. "And, what Filipino party game did you say is like the piñata, and uses a hockey puck?"

"Hockey? Kano, it's called pukpok palayok, which I'll grant you is not easy to pronounce. This is a traditional game; and a clay pot, or palayok, acts as the piñata.

In a similar fashion to breaking the piñata, a player is blindfolded and tries to hit the pot with a bat or a stick, and if he successfully breaks it, out drop coins, candies, and other small prizes—and of course, then it's a mad scramble to pick up as much as you can."

"Sounds like fun, too," said the Kano.

As they walked back in, a few titas, along with the Lola, were in the family room, comfortably seated on the sofas, talking. The television was on, programmed to a Cindy Crawford infomercial for her skin care line. A lively conversation began about her mole.

"You know, you can tell a lot about a person from his or her mole," said Tita Lovely.

'Yes, just look at Cindy Crawford. His mole is right next to her lips, and that's a sign of being talkative. Just look at this infomercial, it's on all the time, and she never stops talking!" laughed Tita Honey.

"I've always liked Marilyn Monroe. Her mole was on her cheek. What does that mean?" asked Tita Ginger.

"I've heard that a mole on the face means that one will be successful in business," Tita Lovely answered. "I guess that applies to her, in some way."

"Yes, moles are very revealing," said the Lola. "I was trying to tell my granddaughter this on her wedding day, but she just brushed off the idea."

"Moles are revealing in what way?" asked Tita Honey.

"You know Ronron's daughter Bekbek?" asked the Lola. "He just had a baby, named Junjun, and she has a mole on his footfoot, I mean foot."

"Yes, of course, Ronron is our cousin, so Bekbek is our niece, which makes his child our granddaughter. Oh, we'll be lolas too!" said Tita Honey.

"Uh, wait a minute," said the Kano as he turned to the Teacher. If Ronron is their cousin, then Bekbek and Junjun are their cousins too—in this case first cousins once and twice removed"

"Kano, you just need to go with the flow when it comes to relationship terms. A cousin is a cousin, but genealogy can get a bit, let's say, creative."

"And what does having a mole on one's foot mean?" asked Tita Lovely.

"If a baby is born with a mole on his foot," said the Lola, "it means she will travel a lot and is a born adventurer."

"Maybe baby Junjun will climb Mt. Pinatubo," said Tita Honey.

"During the next eruption," said Tita Ginger.

"Babies born with a mole near his eye mean she will be easily widowed and if the mole is on his forehead, she will grow up intelligent," said the Lola.

"A mole on the right thigh means prosperity and happiness in marriage," said Tita Ginger.

"And if it's on the left, it means a life of hardship and lack of friendship," said the Lola.

Tita Lovely turned halfway around and pulled down her collar, exposing a mole on the nape of her neck. "You know, I had quite the number of suitors when I was younger," she said slyly. "Can't you tell?"

"You're right about that," said Tita Honey. "All the boys were interested in you when we were growing up. But why are you not showing the mole on your back?"

"My back? Uh, what are you talking about?" Tita Lovely asked, clearly nervous and uncomfortable.

"C'mon, you know. If a mole at your nape makes you popular, a mole on your back makes you lazy. Admit it, you love to sleep every chance you get!" said Tita Honey.

"Ayy," laughed the other titas.

"That's not my problem anymore," protested Tita Lovely, "that's your problem anymore."

"Hey, don't forget about me," said Mr. Mendozas's brother, Dandan, entering into the conversation and clearly enjoying his sixth San Miguel beer. "Just look at this beauty," he said as he proudly pointed to his forehead. "I just can't hide how smart I am."

"A mole in the middle of one's forehead is a sign of great intellect and business success," said Tita Ginger. "What does yours mean?"

All the sisters broke out in raucous laughter.

"*Hay naku,*" said the brother and left the room.

"Haiku?" asked the Kano. "I thought haikus were Japanese."

"Haikus are Japanese poems, but the phrase *hay naku* is Tagalog, and it signals frustration," said the Teacher. "The English translation would be something like 'Oh, my gosh' or 'Oh, dear.' Some linguists say it comes from the phrase *nanay kop o*, which means 'Oh, my mother!' Here, in this family setting, it's mostly in good humor."

"There seem to be a lot of Filipino superstitions regarding moles. Any reason why?" asked the Kano.

"I don't think it's uniquely Filipino," said the Teacher. "Mole superstitions have flourished since ancient times. Chinese astrologers actually believe that the position of moles on the face or body give all kinds of insight into our personalities, our future, even our health. And in Chinese society, moles have something to do with luck."

"There's that luck thing again," said the Kano.

"Here's a little fun fact that has to do with moles, or I should say, does not have to do with moles," said the Teacher.

"Huh?"

"Rolando Dela Cruz, a Filipino, invented mole remover."

"Really?"

"Yes," said the Teacher. "His formula is quite ingenious: an extract from cashew nut, which is common in the Philippines. It can remove moles, and even warts, from the skin without leaving marks."

"Wow, keep that stuff away from Cindy Crawford. It could ruin her career."

"Over the years, I've jotted down some of these mole superstitions as I heard them. I'm not sure," said the Teacher, "if these motivated Mr. Dela Cruz to create his wart removing cream, but here, let me read a few." The Teacher produced a scroll, seemingly out of nowhere.

"You just happen to have a scroll of Filipino mole-ly sayings?" asked the Kano, incredulously.

"Ang Aking Espiritu Ay Filipino," said the Teacher. "*Ako ang iyong guro.*"

"Huh? Did you say 'guru'?" asked the Kano.

"My spirit is Filipino, you know that one. And I am your teacher, or ako ang iyong guro. Therefore, I have to be ready at a moment's notice to instruct and train you properly." He unfurls the scroll and reads it in a British accent, "Hear ye, hear ye, a proclamation about moles to you, the Kano."

Whereas a mole on the back is a sign of laziness; and

Whereas a mole on the stomach is a sign of gluttony and selfishness; and

Whereas a mole on the left chin is a sign of prosperity and many children; and

Whereas a mole on the right chin is a sign of a good heart and a good head for finances; and

Whereas a mole between the two eyes is a sign of being lucky in business; and

Whereas a mole on a man's heart means that he is a flirt; and

Whereas a mole on a woman's heart means she is loyal when in love; and

Whereas a mole on the hand signifies wealth; and

Whereas a mole on the hand signifies thievery; and

Whereas a mole on the heel of a woman signifies that she is stubborn but industrious; and

Whereas a mole on the heel of a man signifies that he is stylish and fond of grooming himself;

Now, hence I, Teacher of the Kano, do hereby proclaim that when it comes to the meaning of moles on one's body, be it the head, torso, arms, legs or feet, the Filipino can pretty much make it mean whatever they want!

"Have mole, will travel," said the Kano.

"Yes, if the mole is on the bottom of one's foot," said the Teacher with a grin.

As the party had been going on for several hours, Mrs. Mendoza grew concerned she hadn't seen her children in a while. She walked into the family room. "Ma, where did my children disappear to?"

"I think I saw them go to the basement, let me check." The Lola walked down the stairs to the basement to look for her grandchildren, but didn't find anyone. "Anak!" she screamed. She heard only silence. "Anak!" This time, she did hear the sound of children—who were trying, unsuccessfully, to keep from laughing out loud.

"Lola, here we are!" they giggled, as they stumbled out of two cardboard boxes.

"Anak, you must be careful. You almost were shipped to the Philippines."

"Teacher, is that a superstition?" asked the Kano.

"Is what a superstition?"

"If you hide in a box in the basement, and your lola discovers you, you'll be shipped to the Philippines?"

"Hah, no, not at all. The Lola was referring to the *balikbayan* boxes the children were hiding in."

"Ballet... box.... I'm sorry, I can't pronounce that," said the Kano.

"Bal-leek-bye-on," said the Teacher.

"Bal-leek-bye-on?" repeated the Kano.

"Yes, that's right. Balikbayan boxes are a relatively new tradition, starting in the 1980s when there was a surge of Filipino workers coming here to the US. *Balikbayan box* roughly translates to 'repatriate box,' and it's a strong, corrugated box that contains items sent by overseas Filipinos, who are known as balikbayans, back home to the Philippines."

"Kind of like a care package?" asked the Kano.

"Yes, sort of. The balikbayan sends things she thinks the recipient will like, even if some of those items can be bought cheaply in the Philippines, like non-perishable food, toiletries, household items, electronics, toys, designer clothing; or, items that might be difficult to find back home," said the Teacher.

"It must be fun and exciting to receive a bal-leek-bye-on box!"

"Yes, and they can be shipped, or brought in person. I remember balancing a number of balikbayan boxes on a luggage cart at the airport as I helped my in-laws depart for a trip to the Philippines," said the Teacher.

"So gift-giving is important to Filipinos?"

"Yes. In the Philippine practice of *pasalubong*, there's an expectation that one bring gifts to family and friends. You could say that the balikbayan box is a modern outgrowth of that tradition."

"Teacher?"

"Yes, Kano?"

"Time to get back upstairs. I'm feeling hungry, and maybe Mrs. Mendoza will pass-a-long some more chicken lollipop to me!"

Unbeknownst to them, the Lola had already gone upstairs. Stepping back into the kitchen, they were surprised to find her in front of the stove, wearing a duster and looking quite serious about the giant bowl of eggs on the counter and the frying pan on the burner. Sounds of cracking eggs and sizzle started to fill the room.

"Lola," asked Beauty, another grandchild and who just wandered into the kitchen, "why are you breaking so many eggs? Are you making a gigantic omelet? There's still food on the table."

"No, I'm not making an omelet; I'm trying to become wealthy."

"Wealthy? You mean, like rich?"

"Of course. Who wouldn't want to be rich?" asked the Lola.

"Are you going to sell your omelets to the neighbors so you can get rich?" asked Beauty.

"Like I said, I'm not making omelets, my dear."

"Then why are you using so many eggs?"

"Because when a person breaks an egg and sees two yolks, she'll become wealthy," said the Lola.

"I guess you haven't seen two yolks yet, huh, Lola?"

"Oh well, never mind. Here, have some peanuts."

"I don't like peanuts," said Beauty.

"They will make you smarter."

"Really?"

An older grandchild, Kitkat, walked in and asked the Lola if she'd seen the spray starch, because she was going to iron an outfit for later in the day.

"It's in the linen closet, on the floor," said the Lola. "Did you already take your bath today?"

"Uh, no. Why, Lola?"

"Make sure you take it before ironing your clothes, otherwise, you'll get sick."

"Are you sure? C'mon, Lola, you can't expect me to believe that, can you?" asked Kitkat.

"Don't take a bath at night, either," said the Lola.

"Lola, if I'm not supposed to take a bath at night or after I iron clothes, I'm going to be *mabaho!*"

The younger grandchild covered her mouth and laughed, as she knew that mabaho meant "smelly" in Tagalog.

"Taking a bath at night can cause anemia or low blood pressure. Even worse is if you sleep with wet hair," said the Lola.

"Do Filipinos ever take showers, Teacher? I mean, all I hear about are baths," said the Kano.

"The words bath and shower are used interchangeably."

"Okay, Lola, tell me what the deal is with wet hair," said Kitkat.

"Sleeping with wet hair can cause blindness or make one crazy."

"I've slept with wet hair before and I'm not blind. Maybe catching a cold has some truth to it, but blindness?"

"*Basta*," said the Lola.

"Did she say 'pasta'?" asked the Kano. "I hope the Lola is going to make some pasta, because I'm starving. Even if she puts Oscar Mayer wieners in it, I'm chowing down."

"Kano, you're a bit skinny for always being so hungry. And for now, you'll stay that way," said the Teacher, "because she did not say 'pasta,' she said 'basta.' *Basta*, not pasta! Basta roughly translates to 'just because' or 'don't ask for details, just do it.'"

"Ooh, I like that. Kind of a Filipino Nike-thing, 'Just do it,'" said the Kano. "Maybe I can use that on Maria."

"Use it? On Maria?" asked the Teacher. "What's that supposed to mean?"

"So I don't have to explain myself. When I tell her something, and if she asks any questions, I'll just say 'Basta.'"

"Kano, you're a pool, er, I mean a fool. It doesn't work that way. And may I remind you—Maria is still a big *if*."

"If?" the Kano asked. "Are you starting to doubt me?"

"Earth to Kano. You've haven't even had a second date. It's questionable if you've had a first. So, don't think about being cute with the word basta, because if you think you're going to order her around or something, believe me, you're not going to win her heart," said the Teacher.

"Well, I didn't exactly mean, I—"

"Kano, if you think you're going to basta Maria, you know what she'll tell you?"

"What?"

"Basta la beesta, baby. Basta la beesta. See you later, Kano!"

The Lola sat down at the kitchen table and invited the children to do the same. "And don't remove earwax at night, or you'll become deaf the following week."

"Lola, you tell us what not to do at night or what not to do when going to bed. Is there something we can do?" asked Kitkat.

"Yes, if you want to be remembered by a friend, put that friend's picture under your pillow when you go to sleep."

"What else?"

"That's about it," said the Lola.

"That's it? That's the only good thing that can happen to someone at nighttime or when going to bed?"

"Yes, mostly, you have to watch out for what not to do."

"Uy. Okay, Lola, I'm ready. What else shouldn't I do?"

"When two dogs bark at night, watch out, there's a ghost."

"Okay, that doesn't seem too unreasonable to believe."

"And, there's something else about wet hair at night."

"Yes, what is it?" asked Kitkat.

"Do not comb it."

"Why?"

"Because if you comb wet hair at night, your parents can die."

"Aah!" screamed Beauty who was still listening in on the conversation.

"Don't eat sour fruits at night either," said the Lola.

"Because…"

"Because this, too, can cause the death of your parents," said the Lola.

"Aah!" the children screamed.

"Wash your feet before going to bed, and don't whistle in the evening. But don't ask me why; even I can't remember," said the Lola, with a laugh.

"Lola," said a little one, "my friend said you shouldn't open an umbrella in the house because it will bring bad luck. Is that true?"

"Partly. If you open an umbrella in the house, it will bring something."

"What?" she asked.

"Centipedes. Centipedes will fall off the ceiling."

"Aah!"

Mrs. Mendoza, who had stepped out momentarily, came back into the kitchen. "Ma!" Failing to get her attention, she said, "Uy!"

"*Ano?*"

"Ma, please, enough with the superstitions. I need to warm up some more *bistek* for our guests. Would you mind relaxing in the living room while I clean up this... this mountain of eggs and get the bistek on?"

"What's bistek?" asked the Kano.

"Beefsteak. It's delicious. Beef and onions cooked in soy sauce. Put it over rice, and you've got a meal fit for a king, as far as I'm concerned."

"Teacher," said the Kano, "Maria will find out quickly that the way to my heart is through my stomach."

"Yes, very quickly."

As the Lola got up from the kitchen table and started for the living room, she was careful not to step over Beauty, the youngest child, who now was lying on the floor, out of fear that if she did step on her, the child would stop growing.

"Hi, Lola," said Marisol, a 17-year-old high school senior, who was sitting on the couch, looking at her phone.

"I heard Marisol, I heard," said the Lola with a big smile as she sat down with her.

"Heard what?"

"You have a boyfriend."

"That's news to me," she said.

"You were seen with a boy who is not Filipino, so of course, that means he's your boyfriend, and we all know about it."

"Her mother couldn't get her to go on a date with so many of our friends' sons, I lost count," called out Mrs. Mendoza from the kitchen. "And now, my niece has done it on her own."

"Sorry to disappoint everybody, but false alarm," said Marisol.

"You look a little tired. And what's that on your cheek?" asked the Lola.

"My cheek?" Marisol asked, startled, rubbing her fingers along her face. "Aah!" she shrieked upon discovering a new pimple.

"Are you in love?" asked the Lola.

"Only if a dermatologist walks through the door," said Marisol, obviously still distressed over her discovery.

"That's why you have a *tigyawat*, a pimple. You're losing sleep because you're in love."

"Lola!"

"Well, regardless of whether you have a boyfriend or if you're in love, you should know a few things about boys, or men, for that matter," said the Lola.

"What should I know, Lola?"

"Do you want to make sure you avoid the liars right away?"

"Of course I do."

"A liar's teeth will be spaced apart."

"Eww."

"Does he have a unibrow?"

"A unibrow? Do you mean does he, if there was a he, have one eyebrow, more or less?"

"Yes."

"Don't worry, I'll be avoiding the unibrowers," said Marisol.

"That's good. People with eyebrows that almost meet easily get jealous. You don't want a jealous boyfriend, do you?"

"No, too much drama for me," she said.

"Make sure you get a good look at his gums too," said the Lola.

"His gums?"

"Yes, if his gums are black, it's another sign that he'll be a jealous type," said the Lola. "How about his hair? Do you like boys with curly hair?"

"Who doesn't?" she said enthusiastically.

"Only those who don't want a moody and temperamental boyfriend," said the Lola. "Is he moody? Do you want a moody boyfriend?"

"Lola, c'mon. You can't mean that, can you?"

"And his head? What kind of a head do you like?"

"A head? I don't think I've ever... I mean... I guess one that's pretty normal, maybe a bit wide," said the granddaughter.

"Wide? That's good; a wide forehead is a sign of intelligence. If his forehead is narrow, he'll be dull," said the Lola. "Watch out for wide shoulders though—because then he'll be lazy."

"I have no problem avoiding boyfriends with a unibrow and black gums. But one with broad shoulders and curly hair? I'm supposed to avoid that, too?" asked the granddaughter, swooning. "*Talaga?*"

"Tagalog? Why did she end her sentence like that?" asked the Kano. "That's kind of like me ending this sentence with the word English. Weird."

"Talaga means 'really.' That's what she said, not Tagalog."

"I don't think I like your type," said the Lola to her granddaughter.

"Lola!"

"But despite what you say, I can see you are in love with this boy, who is not Filipino, but you were seen with him once, so that's why we all know about it. It's okay, you can admit it now."

"Ahh, Lola," said Marisol, resigning herself to the truth, "is it written all over my face?"

"Actually, your fingernails. It's written all over your fingernails. Did you notice all the white spots on your fingernails? It means you are constantly in love," said the Lola.

"Really? I was getting concerned about that. I didn't know what the cause was. Phew! It's just because I'm in love," she said and spun around like a ballerina, in perfect pirouette form.

"So this one you believe, huh?" asked the Lola.

"Just this one," Marisol said with a big grin.

The Lola walked out of the living room, almost tripping over some *burloloys*, or bric-a-brac, and into the garage to fetch some empty magnolia ice-cream containers for baon. "Aah!" she screamed, dropping the plastic containers on the garage floor.

Several people ran into the garage. "Are you okay?"

"Yes, yes, I am. I was frightened by the cats."

"Cats? You mean Frisky?" asked Mrs. Mendoza, who had run to the garage when she heard her mother's scream. "Ma, we've had Frisky for ten years. Do you mean she startled you?" She reached down and picked up the cat up, gently petting her white fur.

"There were two cats here just a minute ago," said the Lola. "Frisky, and a black cat."

"Oh, the black cat. Yes, that's our neighbor's."

"They were fighting with each other, that's why I was afraid."

"Oh, no need to be afraid, Ma, I'm sure they were just playing."

"No, the cats were fighting, I'm sure of it. So that means…" said the Lola, trailing off.

"What?"

"This neighbor with the black cat, do they have children?"

"Yes, a little boy named Jerome. He's in the basement right now, with the other kids."

"Uy. Two neighborhood cats fighting mean the children will soon be fighting one another too," said the Lola.

"Ma, please, you have to stop this."

As they walked back into the living room, Adonis, Mrs. Mendoza's youngest son, came running up from the basement, crying, looking for his mother. "Mom, Mom!" he shouted.

"Anak, what? What is it? Your nose is bleeding, what happened?"

"Jerome punched me in the nose!"

"*Jus ko,*" said Mrs. Mendoza as she tended to the boy with some tissues, which were really paper towels. "Why?"

"I gave him the *usog,*" said the boy.

"Teacher," said the Kano, "a hog? The boys are playing with hogs, with pigs? In the house?"

"Kano, shh. Listen."

"Why did you give him the evil eye?" reprimanded Mrs. Mendoza. "You shouldn't give anyone the evil eye."

"Because he said, he said—"

"What did he say, Anak? It can't be that bad."

"He said you were an aswang!"

"Aah!" screamed the mother. "Why would he say such a thing?"

"It's your *dinuguan.*"

"My dinuguan?"

"Yes, he said you make it from the liver and hearts of young children, not from the innards of a cow, and that's why you are an aswang," said Adonis.

"Next time, use both of your eyes and give him two usogs!" she said, and stormed out of the room.

"Uh, now I get the chocolate pudding thing, Teacher. Tell me about this evil eye superstition," said the Kano.

"It sounds like the children have heard of usog, but don't really know what it means."

"What do you mean?"

"An usog is an affliction, if I can call it that, and can be put upon someone—usually a child, by the greeting, or an evil eye hex, of a stranger."

"Was this evil eye belief something that came from other cultures or influences?" asked the Kano.

"There may be some influence from the Spanish, who have longed believed in the *mal de ojo* superstition," said the Teacher. "Meaning that a look can literally curse people, particularly children, making them sick."

"So, what can happen, or what do people believe can happen?"

"Fever, and sometimes convulsions," said the Teacher. "Or, it could be vomiting and stomach ache. May affect an adult, but it's less common."

"How do you prevent it? Garlic?"

"Garlic? Please Kano, we're not talking American vampires," said the Teacher. "One way is to simply stop a stranger or visitor from a greeting itself. Otherwise, a cursed child can be cured by placing his clothing in hot water and boiling it."

"Hmm, I don't mean to be insensitive, but this does seem odd," said the Kano.

"It's okay. How many Filipinos really believe in usog? I don't know, it probably falls under the attitude of *hindi mo alam* or 'you never know,'" said the Teacher. "And if parents get really anxious, they will ask the visitor or stranger to place saliva on the child and say *"pwera usog, pwera usog"* so as to not become a victim of usog."

"Again, I don't mean to be insensitive, but how much spit, er, saliva, are we talking about?" asked the Kano.

"Just a little on the finger. The idea is to prevent the child from getting overpowered or *upang hindi mausog,"* said the Teacher. "Did you know that the belief of the medicinal benefit of spit goes back to Roman times?"

"Talaga?" asked the Kano.

"Yes. And today, we know that saliva contains enough antimicrobial compounds such as lactoferrin, lactoperoxidase and secretory immunoglobulin A to help prevent infection," said the Teacher. "So you see, we shouldn't be too quick to think another culture's beliefs, or even superstitions, are so completely at odds with our own beliefs. There may be some points of commonality."

"I see what you mean, Teacher," said the Kano.

Adonis seemed pleased with his mother's answer and headed back down to the basement to play with the others. "Who wants to play pool?" he shouted as he got to the foot of the stairs. Typical of children, they soon all forgot what they had been fighting about.

"Teacher, I did notice that beautiful pool table in the basement. Is pool a popular sport among Filipinos? I saw a woman just the other day on TV winning a big tournament on ESPN, and I think she was a Filipina."

"Did they call her the Black Widow?"

"Yes, yes, they did! How did she get that nickname?"

"Her name is Jeanette Lee, and she's not a Filipino. She's American born, of Korean background. She got the name the Black Widow because of how, despite being so nice, she would eat her opponents alive, so to speak."

"Uh, okay, that's great. I'm just a little disappointed, you know, that she's not Filipino, since I've got my Filipino on."

"Don't be, because I'm going to tell you about The Magician," said the Teacher.

"A famous Filipino magician? Ooh, I love magic tricks."

"No, not exactly a magician, because, like the Black Widow, he's a pool player. But, he's Filipino. And he's not just any pool player, and he's not just any great pool player either. This pool player is without question, the greatest pool player that has ever lived."

"Ever lived? Really? Who is he?"

"His name is Efren Manalang Reyes. More commonly known as Efren 'Bata' Reyes, and his nickname is The Magician," said the Teacher.

"Why is he called The Magician?"

"It's not an exaggeration to say that he is head and shoulders above everyone in the sport. His skills are almost unbelievable to watch. He's been described as mindbogglingly, ridiculously good. He's considered the greatest living pool player in the world."

"Wow, a living legend."

"He's won over 70 international titles, including 4 World eight-ball championships."

"I had the Magic 8-Ball when I was a kid," said the Kano. "Oh, it was my favorite toy!"

"Reyes revolutionized how the game is played at the highest level. They say when he went international, players who thought that they were already at the pinnacle of pool playing suddenly became amateurs."

"It sounds like Reyes is to pool what Hussein Bolt, the fastest man in the world, is to sprinting."

"That's a good comparison, Kano. Yet, despite his greatness, Reyes is just as well known for his humility."

"I'm not surprised."

"And in 2003, Efren became the first Asian inductee in the Billiard Congress of America's Hall of Fame."

"Nice!"

"A funny story is told when Reyes was 5 and not tall enough to reach the pool table: He practiced while standing on Coca-Cola cases that he moved around."

"Why is he called Bata? Is that another nickname?"

"Kind of," said the Teacher. "*Bata* is Tagalog for 'kid.' There was an adult at the pool hall who was also named Efren, so the younger one was called bata, or kid, to distinguish them. And, he's sometimes called Efrey."

"Efrey?"

"Yes, it's a combination of Ef from Efren and Rey from Reyes."

"Why am I not surprised," said the Kano.

As the children were now playing nicely in the basement, the Lola and Floribeth went back to the kitchen, and sat down at the vinyl covered table. In the center of the table was a Lazy Susan.

"What's a merry-go-round doing on the table?" asked the Kano.

"Kano, you've never seen one of those before? It's a lazy Susan."

"Ma, I saw you," said Floribeth.

"Saw me what?" said the Lola.

"Sprinkling salt. And not on the food."

"I don't know what you mean," said the Lola unconvincingly.

"When we walked over toward our vinyl-covered kitchen table, you were sprinkling salt here or there, trying not to be noticed."

"I'm just trying to get rid of a few unwanted visitors," said the Lola.

"Ma, nobody here is unwanted."

"Then the salt won't work."

Two boys join them at the table, sitting across from each other, to play a game using pennies.

"Boys, don't do that."

"Aww, can't we stay here and play, Lola?" they asked.

"You can stay here, but don't put those coins on the table," she said.

"I know why, because they're dirty," one of the boys said.

"That's true, they are dirty, so go take a bath," said the Lola.

"Lola!" they shrieked.

"The reason you shouldn't put money or coins on top of the dining table," said the Lola, "is because it attracts bad luck. Soon, all your income will go to food expenses and nothing will be left for other things."

"Boys, that's not true," said Mrs. Mendoza.

"Bahala na," said the Lola.

"Why are there so many superstitions about money?" asked the Kano.

"I'm not sure there are more about money than other things. Maybe just because everyone can use some more of it."

"Do you know any other ones?"

"I've heard a few. Never leave your purse on the floor, or your budget might run low."

"Teacher, I didn't know you used a purse. Then again, I've seen you wearing pink chinellas."

"Kano!"

"Sorry, Teacher."

"If you give someone a wallet or purse as a gift, putting a small amount of money inside means they'll have good luck."

"I do have a birthday coming up," said the Kano.

"Use your right hand when paying with money," said the Teacher, "and the left hand when receiving money."

"Did I tell you I'm a lefty?"

Tres came back into the kitchen, looking for some ketchup.

"Anak, it's in the closet," said Mrs. Mendoza.

Peering into the closet, he asked her, "Should I use the gigantic Price-Club sized ketchup, or one of the hundreds of little ketchup packs from McDonald's?"

"Use a little pack. We don't want to waste anything."

"*Psst. Psst.*"

"Kano, did you just say 'Psst'? When did you learn that?"

"Learn what?"

"*Psst. Psst,*" said the Teacher.

"I haven't learned it, exactly. It sort of just came into my head. I wanted to ask you about it, because I heard the Lola use it before to get somebody's attention."

The Teacher had apparently drifted into a daydream, as he seemed to be distracted and not listening to what the Kano was saying.

"Teacher. Teacher! *Psst. Psst!*"

"*Ano ba?* I mean, what, what is it?"

"Hay naku!" said the Kano. "Wait, what did I just say?"

"Kano, this is amazing. Remember? 'Hay naku' is a phrase used when you're a bit frustrated. Kind of like 'oh, my gosh.'" First, 'psst' and now 'hay naku'!" You're starting to think Filipino. By George, I think you've got it!"

While they were talking, the Lola had walked outside and begun to sweep some leaves that had accumulated on the patio. They followed her.

"Don't tell me, don't tell me, Teacher," said the Kano.

"Tell you what?"

"The Lola is using a, hold on, don't say anything. Uh, she's using Wally's tamborine," said the Kano.

"It's ting-ting. And it's not Wally's."

"Huh? Did you say 'ding-ding'? Is that the doorbell? Should I see who's here?" asked the Kano.

"Kano, I didn't say 'ding-ding.' It's *ting-ting*. And there's no Wally, it's *walis*, as in wahl-eese."

"Wahl-eese Ting-ting is at the door? What a strange name."

"Kano! I thought we went over this. Walis ting-ting is a broom for outside sweeping, and a walis tambo is for—"

"Sweeping the bathroom," said the Kano proudly.

"The bathroom? Well, yes, but it's for any room inside the house. The walis tambo is for sweeping inside the house. Why would you think it's just for the bathroom?"

"Because of the tambo part. Remem-bah? And I don't mean Septem-bah. Tim Tebow Tambo? You know, the bathroom thingy?" asked the Kano.

"Of course I remem-bah, and I don't mean Septem-bah, either. I remember you getting it wrong then, and getting it wrong now!" said the Teacher.

"Getting what wrong, Teacher?"

"Tabo. Tabo is just plain tabo! It's not Tim Tabo, and it's not Tim Tambo."

"Got it," said the Kano. "Tabo. Walis-tabo."

"Uy," said the Teacher as he threw his hands up into the air.

"Ahh, the feel of an ocean breeze and the sounds of waves crashing upon the shore," said the Kano, taking a long, deep breath. "This is more like it, Teacher. Now, don't get me wrong; I didn't mind the line dancing last time, but there's nothing like the smell of saltwater in the air and eating fresh lumpia on the beach."

"Fresh lumpia?" Why do you think you'll be eating fresh lumpia, or, any kind of lumpia, for that matter?"

"Uh, well, you know, when we kind of poof somewhere, after a day of instruction and training, and I sort of tell you about what I've learned, and you give me a… a… treat?"

"A treat? You sound like a dog. Kano, the lumpia is not only masarap, but in this situation, it's all about your journey, your transformation, from being just a kano… to a kano with a deep regard for the Filipino people and a great respect for their heritage and customs," said the Teacher.

"Uh, yes, that's right. I didn't mean to be obnoxious."

"I suppose it just comes natural."

"Teacher!"

"*Ako ay humihingi ng paumanhin,*" said the Teacher. "I'm sorry, that was rude of me. Tell me what you've learned today."

"Humi hingi? Rhymes with thingy? Uh, yes, quite a bit, Teacher; I've learned quite a bit today. I loved being at the birthday par-tay, and watching the kids play traditional Filipino games. How the always fashionable Filipina can use Filipino time to her advantage and be fashionably late. And I learned about how some Filipinos can, well, kind of accept things—what's that expression? I know it's not Bahama mama, but it sort of sounds like it? You know what I mean?"

"Yes, bahala na."

"Yes, that's it. Bahama na. Meaning 'whatever will be will be,' so why should I care if I'm in the Bahamas. Bahama na!"

"Kano! Not Bahama na—it's bahala na."

"Hah, just playing with you, Teacher. But seriously, it's like I can use it for anything. If it rains on my wedding day, bahala na. If my roof blows off during a hurricane, bahala na. If the pizza delivery guy is late and my pie is cold, bahala na. If I forget how to pronounce bahala na—then, bahala na. I can see myself bahala na-ing all day long!"

"I'm glad that you like the phrase and have the general idea behind it, but it's used for situations a little more serious than cold pizza. What else impressed you?"

"I was totally impressed by The Magician, Efren Reyes. I've always wanted to shoot pool, but the closest I've come is swimming in one!"

"What else?"

"Wally's tambourines."

"Huh?"

"The brooms, you know, the sweepers."

"Didn't we address this earlier? Nothing to do with someone named Wally. The sweepers are called the walis tambo and the walis ting-ting, one for indoors, one for outdoors."

"Yes, yes. Again, just kidding with you, Teacher. Where can I buy one? My Swiffer isn't so swifty anymore."

"What about usog and the aswang?" asked the Teacher.

"Oh yea, I'm down with the usogs and aswangs. And moles, too. And aswangs with moles. Cindy Crawford's not an aswang with a mole, is she? I don't think I'll ever look at Cindy the same way."

"More importantly, I hope you never look at Maria the same way, based on all you've been learning, and caring about. Now, here's your treat... er, lumpia shanghai."

CHAPTER 8

SERENADE DE BERGERAC

The Kano nervously approached the front door of Maria's home. He had driven the 20 miles to her home from his, hoping to make amends, and apologize for his childish behavior in the coffee shop.

Ding dong. Ding dong. Maria opened the door, clearly surprised by the Kano's appearance.

"Hi, uh, did you think it was one of your cousins?"

"No, I'm not expecting anyone, especially you! What's this about my cousins?" asked Maria.

"Oh, it was a joke," he said nervously. "You know, the double-name doorbell thing?"

"So you came over here to insult me again! Wasn't your behavior in the coffee shop enough? I don't think so," said Maria, as she slammed the door closed.

The Kano stood at the door, motionless, his head down. Maria was peeking through the window, watching him. Wondering.

"Time for my secret weapon," the Kano thought to himself. He turned decisively and walked off the porch toward his car. Maria was a little disappointed to see him go so quickly. But he didn't go. He opened the trunk, and took out a small guitar. Maria was intrigued.

"What are you doing?" said a voice from the trunk.

"Huh!" Who... who is that?" asked the Kano, startled.

"It's me, Kano! Don't you recognize my voice by now?"

"Teacher? Teacher? Is that you?"

"Yes, of course it's me. Who else would be in your trunk?"

"But I don't see you. I just hear you. That means you must, you just must be a... gho—, gho—"

"Kano, I'm not a ghost! How many times do I have to say that? Now, look in the milk crate you've got here in the trunk, on top of the blanket—what do you see?"

"An egg? Is that a baloot egg? Aah! I mean, is that you, Teacher?"

"Yes, it's me. Now take me out; it's hot in here."

The Kano gently took the egg out of the crate and cupped it in his palms. Maria was still peeking out the window, and thought this all very strange, that the Kano would be speaking to a balut egg, especially because of what happened in the coffee shop. She thought he had lost his mind.

"What did you do, Teacher, shrink yourself to fit inside this egg?"

"No, I'm not in it, it's just my voice."

"Just your voice? Then where are you?"

"I'm really not sure. But I know where you are, and what you are about to do, and so my Filipino spirit was called upon to help you."

"So weird. And what do you think I'm about to do?"

"Well, you've been rejected by your Filipina, you're desperate and you think you're about out of options—so you're going old school, you're going to serenade her."

"I'll give you credit, Teacher, you're pretty sharp. But I don't understand why you're here, and hiding in a baloot, and how you're going to help me."

"Kano, you have some vague, romantic idea of singing to a girl as she looks adoringly down upon you from her balcony, but you don't really know anything about the art of serenading, wouldn't you agree?"

"Uh, yes, I guess I would agree with that."

"It's called *harana* and it's the rather lost tradition of serenading that was common in the old days of the Philippines."

"Harana?"

"Yes, and, although it's thought of as a lone singer and his guitar—"

"Like me," interrupted the Kano excitedly.

"Yes, but that image is more common in the movies that it was in real life."

"I hope it can be common right now!"

"Don't worry, Kano, I'm here to help you. But, in actuality, harana was a bigger social event than just a sole guitarist. He would bring his friends along for encouragement and moral support."

"I think he needed the courage part of encouragement most."

"Yes, I suppose that's right, because not all suitors are good singers. In those cases, he hires a professional," said the Teacher.

"A professional?"

"Yes, called a *haranista*, and if he can get one, a master haranista."

"A master haranista. Cool. Sounds like a coffee barista. Boy, could I use a Starbucks mocha latte vanilla creamo right now."

"Kano! A true master haranista follows a code of honor, called *magalang at maginoo*."

"Magala... er, Mr. Magoo... sorry, Teacher, I can't pronounce that."

"Don't worry, just know that it's the epitome of chivalry. Anyway, there's a sort of formality to the harana, as it progresses from a beginning to an end."

"An end? Like the guy gets the girl?"

"Kano, be nice! Serenading is not about getting, it's about giving. Now, first, there's the calling or announcement, and this is called the *panawagan*. A song like 'Dungawin Mo Hirang,' which means 'Look Out the Window, My Beloved' may be sung."

"How romantic," said the Kano, tapping his heart with the palm of his hand.

"Then, it's the proposal stage."

"Oh yeah, baby, just what I want to hear: time to ask for Maria's hand."

"Kano, not a marriage proposal, but it's when the haranista, or singer, is invited into the family home and sings about the virtues he values in a woman," said the Teacher.

"I'm swooning."

"Then, it's time for her to respond, by song, which will indicate some interest, or no interest at all."

"Can someone say 'nail-biter'?"

"Yes, it can be stressful," said the Teacher. "If she declines his invitation, he'll sing something like 'Ako 'y Isa Na Ngayong Sawi,' which means 'I am now brokenhearted.'"

"Do you have a tissue? This is all so touching, I'm about to cry," sniffled the Kano.

"It all ends with the *pamaalam*, or farewell song, to apologize for any inconvenience he may have caused."

The sound of a blowing nose rings out. "So touching, just so touching," the Kano said as he continued sniffling, tissue in hand.

"Pull yourself together, Kano; Maria is still peeking out from the window, and looking puzzled at your behavior."

"Right, don't worry, I'm good," he said as he pulled himself together.

"Kano, have you heard of Cyrano de Bergerac?"

"Hmm, is she Filipino?"

"Kano, it's not a she, it's a he. And it's a play. De Bergerac was a soldier in the French Army and he was a skilled fighter and gifted poet. But, he had one problem."

"One problem?" asked the Kano.

"Yes, he had an extremely large nose."

"Gosh, so much attention to noses."

"His large nose affected his self-confidence, and prevented him from expressing his affection for Roxanne, the woman he loved."

"Teacher, are you saying I have a big nose?"

"Your nose is fine."

"Just fine?" asked the Kano.

"Yes, it's fine."

"Fine like in fine dining, or fine like in 'Fine, we'll eat McDonald's tonight since nobody made dinner'?"

"Kano, can't you get your mind off of food, ever?"

"Like I told you before, I'm a growing boy."

"Anyway, to make a long, rather complicated story short, Cyrano actually helps another gentlemen win the heart of Roxanne, as it was he whom she thought she loved, and not Cyrano."

"So beautiful, so chivalrous," sniffed the Kano. "How'd he do it?"

"Since Christian, this man she loved, was rather, well, uneducated and foolish, Cyrano became his voice—through writing letters to her, as well as during a dramatic moment under her balcony."

"Under the balcony? Hmm, this is starting to sound a little bit familiar."

"Yes, this is when Cyrano hides in the bushes and whispers to Christian, who is looking up to Roxanne, what to say to win her heart."

"Ahh, okay, I got it. You're going to be the Cyrano guy and I'm going to be the Christian guy."

"Yes."

"Teacher, are you saying I'm uneducated and foolish, like Christian was?"

"Kano!"

"Okay, what do you want me to do?"

"Can you lip sync?" asked the Teacher.

"Can I lip sync? Can you say 'Millie Vanilli'?" asked the Kano before breaking off into song. "Girl, you know it's true, ooh, ooh, ooh, I love you."

"Kano, we don't have time to play games. Can you lip sync or not?"

"Yes, I can lip sync; why?"

"Because you certainly can't sing."

"Hey, why are you saying I can't sing?"

"Well, before that awful Milli Vanilli rendition, I'd previously heard you sing in the shower."

"Teacher, have you been Espiritu-ing in my shower? Eww, I feel so violated."

"Kano, don't be silly. I am a man of integrity, not to mention a weak constitution. I've just heard your, let's call it, your shower voice, wafting about."

"I don't think it's so bad."

"Aren't you trying to win Maria back? I don't think she's going to fall head over heels over 'not so bad'."

"So what's your plan?"

"Pull yourself together and go back on the porch. Place me, er, this balut egg, behind the porch post, out of view and start playing the guitar. You can play the guitar, can't you? I assume so, since you brought one here."

"Well, sort of, uh, not exactly—I thought I could just strum and sing."

"Okay, that's fine—just strum, and I'll handle the rest."

"And I'll lip sync?"

"Yes, remember, I'm your Cyrano, your master barista… er, haranista, I'm your master haranista."

"But I don't know what you're going to sing. How will I move my lips? I'll look ridiculous!"

"Don't worry about it, just start moving your lips, and I'll sing. You'll catch on."

"Did you serenade your asawa?"

"No, I have a terrible voice."

"A terrible voice? Then why are we doing this Serenade de Bergerac thing if you can't sing? And why am I talking to an egg? This is *so* weird."

"Kano, you're getting my Filipino spirit voice, not my regular kano voice. Don't worry, it's good; you won't be embarrassed."

Maria had been observing all of this through the window. She saw the guitar, and what appeared to be a conversation the Kano was having with a balut egg. She thought he was working up the nerve to eat some balut in front of her, to make up for the coffee shop incident, but was unsure of why he had a guitar.

Situating himself and the balut egg as the Teacher suggested, the Kano rang the doorbell, backed up on the porch, and started to strum. Maria giggled and, assuming she was about to be serenaded, went upstairs to her bedroom, opened the window, and leaned out to see the Kano below.

Continuing to strum his guitar, the Kano looked up at Maria and started moving his lips. But no sound came out of the balut egg! Smiling nervously, he talked out of the side of his mouth toward the egg. "*Psst*, Teacher, Teacher. *Psst*. You're not singing, Maria is looking very confused."

"Kano, I was singing, but my voice couldn't make it through the egg shell. I think we have a feather problem."

"A feather problem?"

"Yes, I don't think my voice is getting out through the porous shell openings, because the embryonic duck's feathers in this egg are bit thick."

"Embryonic duck feathers? Please, Teacher, don't remind me," said the Kano, nauseated. "I think I have a weak constitution too. Ohh."

"Kano, keep your poise. Keep your focus. Keep your lunch down. It's okay, I just need to concentrate some more, more focus, more focus, and ahh, good, good, I broke through, Kano. I broke through. Keep strumming, and start moving your lips, Maria is watching. Everything is going to be okay."

And it was more than just okay. Because the Teacher's voice did break through—in song so beautiful it would make any master haranista proud. The Kano was proud too, as Maria's family had joined her at the window, and they were all watching, and smiling, and enjoying his public display of affection.

"Okay, I believe you, Michael, I believe that you're sorry about the coffee shop," Maria happily shouted from the second floor window.

Relieved, the Kano couldn't hold back his joy while he continued to serenade her. "And I guess that's why you brought balut with you," she said, "you're going to eat it to prove your sincerity."

The Kano smiled nervously at Maria while he continued to lip synch—and with a slight turn of his head and shift of his eyes, looked toward the Teacher, or more accurately, toward the balut egg. He knew what he had to do.

"Uh-oh," said the Teacher. "I think we've got a feather problem."

CHAPTER 9

AND BABY MAKES THREE

Before going to bed that evening, still feeling playful after his serenade debut, the Kano felt stirred to have some fun with the Teacher the next morning. He would rise at 3:30 a.m., a full 90 minutes before the Teacher would be present, arrange his bed and pillows as if he were sleeping and get himself ready for the day. When the Teacher pulled down the covers to wake him, seeing nobody in bed, he would then jump out of the closet he was hiding in and yell *boo!*, to really play up the 'ghost thing.' He set the alarm for 3:30 a.m. and went to bed.

"Aah!" shrieked the Kano as he slipped into bed, and then immediately jumped out, pointing back at it. "What are you doing here? And why are you hiding in my bed?"

"I heard about your plans," said the Teacher.

"What? How could you… I, I just don't understand."

"Get used to it, Kano."

"Used to what?"

"Not understanding," said the Teacher as he got out of the bed.

"Not understanding what?"

"Not understanding me, or my ways, but more importantly, your Filipina. You'll never understand her completely. Love her completely, yes. Understand her completely? Well, that's a whole other story. And I'm not talking about Taglish."

"You mean this in a good way, right?" asked the Kano.

"In the best way."

"Okay, now that we've had our bro moment, can you kindly disappear?"

"Since you've summoned me by your thought waves, and I'm here, I, uh, I don't really know how to leave. It just happens naturally. And right now, it's not happening," said the Teacher.

"What about using the secret weapon, you know, Septem-bah?"

"That's the nuclear option, as they say. We go there only as a last resort. Why don't you lie down in bed, and I'll sing you a lullaby," said the Teacher. "Then when you're asleep, and your mind is resting, I'll probably just poof out."

"What? A lullaby? I'm a grown man. Teacher, are you losing it?"

"Not just any lullaby, but 'Uyayi,' the Philippine lullaby."

"You ya way? Is that the Filipino version of 'My Way'? I did it you ya way, for what is a manny, er, a man—"

"Kano!"

"Sorry, Teacher."

The Teacher began to sing. "*Matulog ka na, bunso, Ang ina mo ay malayo, At hindi ka masundo, May putik, may balaho.*"

"What does it mean?" asked a drowsy Kano, struggling to keep his eyes open.

"It translates to 'Sleep now, youngest one, your mother is far away, and she can't come for you, there's mud, there's a swamp.'"

"Not exactly rock... a... rock... a... bye... bae... bee." And with that and a long, lingering yawn, the Kano was sound asleep.

"Uy," said the Teacher. Poof! He vanished into thin air.

Bzz. Bzz. Bzz. It was 5 a.m.

"Rock a bye babe... baby rock," mumbled the Kano, as he reached for the alarm clock, still half-asleep.

"Magandang umaga, Kano.... Good morning, rise and shine. Time to rub that sand out of your eyes," said the Teacher.

"Uy," said the Kano. "Is it really 5 a.m. already? Oh, boy, did I have some dream last night."

"A dream?" asked the Teacher.

"Yes, I dreamed that I was like Grasshopper in the movie Kung Fu, and instead of learning karate, I was being instructed in The Way of the Filipino with my master, like the real Grasshopper learned Kung Fu with his master, and, I... uh, I... oh boy, that wasn't a dream, was it? Teacher!"

"The real world is far better than the dream world, Kano."

"This thing between you and me, though—this isn't exactly the real world."

"If you want it to be real between you and Maria, then yes, this thing of ours is very real. We must forge ahead. C'mon, let's go downstairs," said the Teacher.

The Teacher poured the Kano a cup of hot coffee and positioned the flip chart closer to the kitchen table where he was sitting. "Let's see what kind of progress you're making."

"I'd like to start making progress on getting some more beauty sleep," said the Kano, "and don't go there, I can already read your mind—my morning face is just that, my face in the morning."

"Kano, soon, it will be time for you to mano po, and take the lumpia shanghai from my hand—maybe. But, only if you stay focused and disciplined can you expect to get Maria back. Or at least get started on the road to a real relationship with her."

"Yes, you're right. I'm sorry about that," said the Kano. "Mano po, I'm ready to go."

"Good. So far, you have learned many things about the Filipino people. Things you did not know just a few short days ago. Geography, history, and early US immigration; you've observed their life at home and at celebrations like weddings and birthday parties. You're clued in to some mannerisms that are common," said the Teacher. As he looked up and lip-pointed to nowhere in particular he said, "Hmm, what might be something interesting for you to know that I haven't shared yet? Ahh, yes, yes, Salonga," he said while nodding his head and stroking his chin. "Salonga. Have I mentioned Lea Salonga?"

"What's that, Teacher? Salongpas? Did you say 'Salongpas'? Those pain relief patches? Were they invented by a Filipino too? Oh, good, give me one; my back is killing me from all this Espiritu we've been doing."

"Kano, no, not Salongpas, Salonga. *Ga.* Lea Salonga, the famous Filipina singer and Broadway actress!"

"Got it, check, Lea Salongpas, er, Salonga."

"Kano, check for what? I haven't told you about her yet. By the way, you haven't written anything down, or taken notes or made a list of the things you've learned during these past few days," said the Teacher, a bit exasperated.

"Some of us don't need to write it down, it's all up here, in the mental safe," said the Kano, tapping the side of his head with his index finger.

"Are you sure you know the combination?"

"Teacher, I won't dignify that comment with a response."

"Anyway," said the Teacher, "her full name is Maria Lea Carmen Imutan Salonga, and she was born in 1971."

"Why does she have so many names?"

"Kano! How many times have we talked about Filipinos, and names, and middle names and second middle names, and—"

"Teacher, sorry; yes, I remember, it's all right up here," said the Kano, tapping on the side of his head again.

"Uy. Her big breakthrough was getting the lead role of Kim in the Broadway musical *Miss Saigon*. She was only 18."

"Wow, so young."

"I think she's been instrumental in raising awareness of Filipinos among Americans. She was the first Asian woman to win a Tony Award, the first Filipino artist to sign with an international record label, and one of the best-selling Filipino artists of all time."

"The Philippines must be proud of her," said the Kano.

"She's a great source of pride, I'm sure. She received a Presidential Award of Merit from President Corazon Aquino, and she was named one of People Magazine's 50 most beautiful people."

"I'm glad she's created such a positive image for the Filipino people."

"She sure has. Oh, and she was the singing voice for two Disney Princesses, Jasmine in *Aladdin* and Fa Mulan in *Mulan*, and she was named a Disney Legend just a few years ago."

"Loved those movies!"

"Some inside baseball here, but our nephew, Lee, actually played the role of Tam when *Miss Saigon* opened on Broadway some years back."

"Really? Wow!"

"Yes, he's my sister-in-law's son. And, believe it or not, a couple of years later, his sister Melanie stepped in to play the role."

"But in the play, isn't Tam a boy?"

"Yes, but at that age, being so little, it really didn't matter. Plus, she'd been around the set for a couple of years, so it all probably seemed kind of normal for her." The Teacher refilled the Kano's coffee cup. "Kano, I've got a surprise for you today. We're going to pay a visit to the Lola and learn about some interesting beliefs and superstitions concerning pregnancy, babies, and children," said the Teacher as he wrote *Pregnancy* on the flip chart.

"Exciting! Oh, I wish I could meet Lola for real. Is there anything I should know in advance of our visit? Any traditions or superstitions you want to share now, Teacher?"

"I'll be happy to share a few, but I think I kind of created a brand new tradition with the birth of our first child," laughed the Teacher.

"Really? Go on, what happened?"

"I must have misunderstood my wife, because I thought she told me it was a Filipino tradition for the parents to be at the hospital while the mother was in labor," said the Teacher.

"It's not?"

"No, I guess it's not. When my wife went into labor, I called my parents and, of course, told them about this sacred Filipino tradition that both sets of grandparents go to the hospital to wait. As my parents did not want to be culturally insensitive, thinking that my in-laws would be at the hospital, they went. Somewhere along the line, my brother heard about this sacred, time-honored Filipino tradition, and he showed up at the hospital too, wanting to show respect to my mother- and father-in law, immigrants from the Philippines."

"Go on," encouraged the Kano.

"Well, my wife was in labor for a *long* time—in fact, all night! My parents were wondering where my wife's parents were. So was I, until my wife said, "What Filipino tradition are you talking about?"

"Uh-oh, lost in translation, as the saying goes. In the end, we all laughed about it, and my parents were there to see me, in hospital gown and cap, because after 24 hours of labor, a Csection had to be performed and I had gowned up for the OR."

"That's a funny story," said the Kano.

"Okay, back to your training. Like I said, we're going to visit the Lola today, because her granddaughter and husband are visiting, and they have some exciting news."

"Exciting news? And we're going to learn about pregnancy and babies today? Teacher, you're not very good at keeping a secret," said the Kano.

"Ready?" said the Teacher.

"Ready."

"Ang Aking Espirito Ay Filipino, Ang Aking Espirto Ay Filipino," they both said in unison. "Ang Aking Espiritu Ay Filipino."

"Poof!" Instantly, they were transported to the Lola's living room and heard the sounds of ding dong, ding dong.

"Who would have thought Dingdong was such a popular name," said the Kano.

"It's the doorbell you... Kano!" said the Teacher.

"Kumusta?" said the Lola as she greeted her granddaughter, Mona Lisa, and her husband, Pedro, with a beso, or kiss on the cheek.

"Hello, Lola," they said together. "You heard the exciting news?"

"Hey, that's the bride and groom, from the wedding," said the Kano.

"Yes I did hear the news," said the Lola, "and it's so good that you're here. I have so much to tell you." She led them into the living room, and lip-pointed to the big couch—and momentarily stepped into the kitchen to bring back some refreshments. She joined the grandchildren on the sofa.

"Lola, are you going to tell us how to have a lucky baby?" asked Mona Lisa with a big smile.

"Maybe, but put that thought aside right now. I have more important things to tell you."

"More important than luck, Lola? Like what, baby superstitions?"

"Do you think a painful delivery is a superstition?" she asked.

"Uh, no, no," she said. "That's pretty common, I'd guess. Is that what you want to tell me about?"

"If it's a painful delivery, it will be a boy. And, if it's an easy delivery, it will be a girl."

"I guess I will just have to have a girl," said Mona Lisa.

"Teacher, that wasn't exactly the case for you… er, your wife, right? I mean, her labor was difficult but it wasn't a boy that came out!"

"You're right about that. We thought our daughter was a boy until she was a girl."

"You thought she was a boy until he was a girl?" chuckled the Kano. "See, I'm getting this he/she thing now."

"The only thing you're getting is annoying," said the Teacher.

"Now," said the Lola to her visitors, giving them a pen and pad of paper she had grabbed from the end-table cabinet, "you'll need to take notes."

"Lola, we just came to visit you, not have a lesson in Filipino baby superstition."

"Let's begin. First, do not have your picture taken, or you will suffer a miscarriage."

"Lola!"

"Did you eat ginger while you and Mr. Wonderful were trying to conceive?"

"Well, I guess so, I mean, yes, you know how good mom's *arroz caldo*, chicken *tinola*, and *tinola manok* is," said Mona Lisa.

"Uy, start praying. Now your baby will be born with an extra finger or toe."

"Lola, please, you'll give us back luck."

"And watch your step. If you fall down hard, you will deliver a hair-lipped baby."

"Hah," laughed Mona Lisa, "that one is funny."

"Don't laugh at these things. It will bring bad luck. Have you had your hair cut recently? Your hair looks very long."

"I have an appointment next week."

"Don't go! Your baby will be born hairless!"

"Lola, you must stop saying these things. Anyway, what's wrong with a bald baby?"

"Let me look at your stomach." She got up off the couch and took a few steps back to better examine her granddaughter's belly. Hmm, it's a little too early, but as time goes on, if your stomach becomes rounded, you'll have a girl, and if it's pointed, you'll have a boy."

"Well, it's a 50-50 chance either way. That sounds more like statistics than superstition, Lola."

The Lola notices a string of pearls on her granddaughter's neck, and is noticeably concerned.

"Lola, what is it?" she asked. "You suddenly look worried."

"I, uh, oh no," she said, continuing to gaze at the string of pearls.

"Lola, are you okay? What's the matter?"

Lola moved toward her granddaughter, and purposely tripped over a karoke microphone that was on the floor, stumbling onto the couch. She deliberately positioned her body to lie across her granddaughter and husband, who had remained sitting. Looking up to Mona Lisa, she said, "My, isn't that a lovely string of pearls."

"Lola, are you okay? You just had a bad fall. Are you sure you didn't break anything? Why are you staring at my necklace?"

"Can I rub your pearls? I heard it's good for luck."

"What isn't good for luck?" asked the Kano.

Lola reached for the pearls and began to rub a few beads between her thumb and forefinger. "Lovely, lovely," she said. Then, abruptly, she pulled down, hard enough to break them off her granddaughter's neck, and jumped off the couch, happy at her catch.

"Lola, what's going on here?" shrieked Mona Lisa, obviously distressed.

"You can thank me in eight months," she said proudly, holding her catch up in the air.

"Thank you? For what?"

"For saving your baby's life. Don't you know that if a pregnant woman wears a necklace or choker, the umbilical cord of her baby will also be wound around its neck?"

"Lola, this is starting to go too far. I mean, if you want to tell me your superstitions, that's, I guess, I guess that's fine. But you can't ruin my jewelry!"

Lola sat back on the couch, positioning herself between the couple. Looking at Mona Lisa she asked, "Do you promise not to wear necklaces or chokers while you are pregnant with my great-grandchild?"

Ignoring the question, she responded, "Lola, we were having a conversation like this before I got married. About superstitions and all. Do you remember?"

"Did you say 'Remem-bah'? Oh, uh, forget I said that. I'm too tired to line dance today," said the Lola. "But, I do remember that you didn't think my advice was so accurate, did you?" She looked at Pedro with a bit of a scowl.

"Lola, Pedro and I love each other. All those things you were worried about, they just didn't happen."

"I guess you're right," said the Lola as she got up and walked out of the room and into the kitchen.

"Mona Lisa, why doesn't your Lola like me?" complained the husband.

"It's not that she doesn't like you," she whispered back, "it's because she doesn't think anyone is good enough for me."

The Lola came back with some garlic and vinegar. "Oh, don't mind me," she said as she placed them on the window sill.

"Garlic? This has something to do with vampires, doesn't it?" asked Mona Lisa.

"Now that you bring it up, yes; I'm making sure vampires won't eat your baby while you're pregnant."

"Lola!"

"Vampires?" asked the Kano. "Teacher, are Filipinos big fans of *Twilight*? Talk of vampires came up during our first visit at the Mendoza home."

"I don't know if Filipinos are fans of *Twilight* more than anyone else, but I do know that the aswang is part of Filipino folklore," said the Teacher. "Again, it's a vampire ghoul-like beast, and its legend can be traced to the Spanish colonists."

"Are aswangs afraid of sunlight?"

"No, they are not harmed by sunlight. And they can be friendly, like a good neighbor, and not harm you. There's a Filipino saying that goes something like better an aswang than a thief because if you're friends, you won't become one of their victims as they look to steal food. Aswang stories vary greatly throughout the Philippines, and there are lots of regional names for them besides *aswang*. By the way, if you want to spot an aswang, just look into its eyes. If your reflection is upside-down, it's definitely an aswang. You could also go *tuwad* on them."

"Tuwad?"

"Yes, you bend over and look at the person from between your legs, upside down. If their image is different, it's an aswang," said the Teacher.

"I can't imagine an aswang even noticing."

Happily grabbing a book from the bookshelf, Lola said, "Oh, here, take a look at this scrapbook I made."

Paging through it, Mona Lisa asked curiously, "Why is everyone in this scrapbook so *guapo* and *maganda*, so handsome and pretty? And who are they? I don't recognize anyone. What is this, a beautiful people book?"

"Yes, it is," said the Lola as she did a little dance. "Now, you will give birth to a beautiful baby, because you looked at pictures of beautiful people."

"Beauty is in the eye of the beholder," she protested.

"You're telling me," said the Lola as she looked disapprovingly at her granddaughter's husband.

"They say if you can't beat them, join them. Okay, Lola, tell me some more things I need to watch out for since I'm pregnant."

The Lola smiled and sat down on the couch again, deliberately squeezing herself in between the couple, not paying any attention to Pedro.

"Oh, I'm so happy you're seeing things my way granddaughter. Okay, where shall we begin? No sitting on stairs, no eating of two bananas, and do not share your food with anyone—not even you-know-who," she said, gesturing with a slight turn of the head toward the husband.

"Are you going to tell me why I should not do these things?"

"Of course. If you sit on the stairs, your delivery will be difficult. You don't want a difficult delivery, do you?"

"Well, no. But—"

"And are you ready to have twins?"

"Uh, well if that's what—wait, why?"

"Eating two bananas means delivering two babies, twins."

"Oh, that's funny. What do I need to eat to guarantee twin girls?" laughed Mona Lisa.

"Aren't you going to ask me why you shouldn't share food with this one?" asked the Lola, lip-pointing at Pedro but not looking his way.

"I've been too hungry to share my food. Why, what will happen if I do?"

"You'll cause spells of drowsiness, dizziness, and vomiting to the person you share your food with."

"Maybe I'll do that when we're having crabs. Because as soon as I get the meat out, he steals it from my plate," said the granddaughter, trying to give a look of love to her husband, while the Lola moved her head from side to side to block the gesture.

"Crabs?" shrieked the Lola.

"Yes, crabs. Why are you so concerned?"

"Let him eat the crabs, because if you do, your baby will be born with six fingers!"

Smiling, the husband said with a grin, not believing any of Lola's warnings, "I'll risk drowsiness, dizziness, and vomiting for the sake of our baby," feeling he got one over on his Lola-in-law.

"See, Lola? Pedro would do anything for me. Isn't that right, *mahal*?"

"Mahal?" asked the Kano to the Teacher.

"It means 'my dear,' 'my loved one,' something like that."

"Oh, you say he would give up anything?" asked the Lola, glaring at the husband.

"Of course. Isn't that right, Pedro?"

"Anything," he replied. "Anything for my mahal."

"What about Thursday nights?" asked the Lola. "Would you give up Thursday nights?"

"Uh, uh, Thursday nights? What about them?" said the husband, visibly nervous.

"Isn't Thursday nights your... bowling nights?" asked the Lola, drawing out the word bowling.

"Uh, yes, sometimes, I mean, yes, you know, I'm in the league, and the top bowler on the team, and the guys count on me to—"

"Oh Lola, Pedro would give up bowling for me in a second. Isn't that right, Pedro? Pedro? Pedro!"

"Uh, sure, you know I would, but the tournament is coming up and, you know, the team needs me and—"

"Uy!" said Mona Lisa.

"Teacher, at Maria's party there was a lively exchange between a few of the men—apparently they are on competing bowling teams. It got pretty heated! Is bowling a popular sport or pastime among Filipinos?"

"It is for some. My asawa and I used to go bowling occasionally with other Filipino couples. Boy, talk about enthusiasm and high fives, even for a spare! I'd bet that Paeng Nepomuceno probably has something to do with the interest in bowling."

"Who's she? Or is she a he?" asked the Kano.

"You could say that he is the Michael Jordan of bowling. Rafael Paeng Nepomuceno is to bowling what Tiger is to golf, Oprah is to talk shows, or Tom Brady is to quarterbacks. I think it's safe to say he is the greatest bowler in the history of the world!"

"Wow, that's saying something."

"Oh yeah, it's like he's not even human. Been bowling for over 40 years—he's now a lolo, but can still make sure it's a *no-no* when it comes to gutter balls!"

"Hah."

"Anyway, he's been the youngest world champion, the oldest world champion, and a prolific champion of bowling tournaments too many to name. He's listed in the *Guinness Book of World Records*, and the Philippine Sportswriter Association named him the Athlete of the Century and the Athlete of the Millennium."

"Impressive!"

"He's been bestowed honors by five different Filipino presidents, from Marcos to Arroyo. And, if you visit the

International Bowling Museum and Hall of Fame in Texas, you will be greeted by a big picture of Paeng in the entrance hall."

"Breaking a hundred doesn't sound like such a big deal for me anymore," said the Kano.

"Another notable Filipino bowler is Olivia Bong Coo," said the Teacher.

"Bong?" laughed the Kano, but quickly regained his poise. "Sorry," he said, while clearing his throat.

"Yes, she's retired now, but she has won more tournaments and trophies that I can count. She is a four-time world champion and, like Paeng, she's in the *Guinness Book of World Records*, with the added distinction of being the first Filipino athlete listed in the encyclical."

"I once went bowling and didn't even throw a gutter ball. Love those bumpers!" said the Kano.

"Bong is considered the most bemedalled Filipino athlete, according to the Athletes Incentives Act of 2001, and she's known as Asia's Bowling Queen," said the Teacher, turning his attention back to the Lola and her guests.

"Lola, I'm sure my very, very loving husband would drop his bowling ball on his foot if I asked him to; isn't that right, Pedro?" grimaced Mona Lisa.

"Yes; yes, dear."

"Granddaughter, can you stand up for your Lola?"

"Of course," she said, while getting up from the couch.

"Now, start walking."

Mona Lisa started to walk, taking a step with her right foot. "It's a girl, it's a girl!" said the Lola.

"How do you know that?"

"Because when you stood up to walk, you started with you right foot. Had you started with you left, you'd be having a boy."

"How about if a pregnant woman eats lunch; will anything bad happen?" said the husband, trying to be noticed, but also getting hungry.

Ignoring him, the Lola looked toward her granddaughter and said, "When you have cravings, you must not deny yourself, because if you do, your child will salivate profusely and will be prone to vomiting. How far along are you?" she asked.

"About six weeks. Why?"

"Have you cried?"

"I did read *The Notebook* last week, and of course I cried."

"Ayy!"

"What's wrong, Lola?"

"You're going to give birth to a crybaby. Uy."

"Teacher, there sure are a lot of superstitions regarding pregnancy, aren't there?" asked the Kano.

"Yes. With most Filipino superstitions, these evolved a long time ago, and they have been passed down from generation to generation, one lola at a time. But, now, most of these are believed, even if they are not truly believed, just to be safe, just in case."

The Lola had prepared a lunch, so they all moved into the kitchen and sat down at the table.

"Teacher, I'm not sure if I'm seeing this right," said the Kano.

"What do you mean?"

"The utensils. They are eating with a fork and a spoon. For me, I use a fork by itself, or a fork and knife combo, or a spoon by itself. But, I don't think I've seen the fork and spoon combo before."

"Yes, well, it's a very common way for the Filipino to eat. I had the same reaction at first. I didn't say anything, just observed. But then I gave it a try. And now I prefer it. Certainly works better when you're eating rice, standing and holding the plate in front of you. Less rice falling to the table, or to the floor."

"Now, Mona Lisa, I know you love pork, but I haven't prepared any today; nor should you eat pork throughout your pregnancy," said the Lola.

"I'm afraid to ask why."

"Because if you eat pork, you may give birth to a baby that looks like a pig."

"Lola!"

"And stay away from eggplant."

"Why? Will my baby have an eggplant-shaped mole somewhere on her body?"

"Not a mole, but a violet discoloration on its skin. But, if the baby does have a mole, even an eggplant shaped one, that would be good luck," said the Lola.

"Mmm, Lola, I love your *adobo*."

"Adobe? Did she say 'adobe'?" asked the Kano. "Is this one of those Spanish colonization holdovers—you know, she's complimenting her Lola on her adobe-style house?" Continuing, the Kano went into dictionary mode: "Adobe, noun. A sun-dried brick made of clay and straw, in common use in countries having little rainfall; a yellow silt or clay, deposited by rivers, used to make bricks; a building constructed of adobe."

"That's wonderful, it really is," said the Teacher. "If we were talking about Lola's house! But we're talking about her adobo, her chicken adobo, not her chicken adobe."

"Ahh, I see; sorry," said the Kano.

"But you're right about a Spanish connection. Filipino adobo comes from the Spanish *adobar*, which means 'marinade' or 'a sauce or seasoning.' It's a popular dish, and easy to cook. Even I can cook it, although my asawa makes the best. You can use meat, seafood, or vegetables and marinate them in vinegar, soy sauce, and garlic; then brown and simmer. Simple and delicious."

"Especially with rice," suggested the Kano.

"Especially," said the Teacher.

"I'm glad you like my adobo. Here, have some more rice. Now, tell me, do you know what to do after the baby is born?"

"Well, I haven't thought about it exactly," said Mona Lisa. "I mean, I guess I'll just do what comes natural."

"Make sure to give your newborn *ampalaya* juice before the first feeding to improve her appetite and prevent his becoming choosy or finicky about food as she grows up," said the Lola.

"What's ampalya juice?" asked the Kano.

"It comes from a tropical plant found in Asia, and you'll hear it referred to as bitter melon or bitter gourd. It does have a bitter taste, but I've had it many times and rather enjoy it. Then again, I like broccoli rabe, so a little bitter, a little better, with me. Anyway, the fruit or juice is said to prevent a number of diseases, disorders, and infections."

"Well, I'm not sure," said Mona Lisa. " I'd rather not give my baby ampalaya, Lola; I don't like it myself."

"Suit yourself. I'm just trying to pass on the wisdom from one generation to the next."

"I appreciate that, Lola. Any other gems?"

"I'm sure you don't want to have morning sickness, do you?"

"Of course not, what woman would?"

"Well then, just jump over your husband, and your morning sickness will transfer to him," said the Lola, lip-pointing toward her husband Pedro, who had returned to the living room and was starting to nod off to sleep on the couch.

"Uh-huh. What's that about morning sickness?" he asked.

Laughing, his wife replied, "We were just saying that you love me so much, you'd take my morning sickness if you could."

"Uh, yes, of course I would, I would," he said and drifted back off to sleep.

"You know about usog, right?" asked the Lola.

"Hey, Teacher, I know about usog," said the Kano. "Remember? Pretty impressive, if I must say so myself."

"Well, since no one else is saying impressive, I guess you will have to say it yourself."

"Yes, Lola, mom has talked about the usog before. The evil eye, right?"

"Yes, here's some lipstick," said the Lola. "Put a dot of this on your baby's forehead after she's born to keep away evil forces."

"How will it do that, keep away evil forces?"

"I haven't the slightest idea," said the Lola.

"Uy," said Mona Lisa.

The Teacher and the Kano are standing on the side of a beautiful cliff, looking over a wide, picturesque river. "Pretty nice, huh?" asked the Teacher.

"Yes, this is very nice. But I do think the beach is just perfect for our Teacher-Kano what-have-you-learned moments, like now. Do you need to avoid the beach, Teacher? Too much ozone? Do you have a sunburn concern?"

"Kano, I can't get sunburn because I'm a—"

"A ghost! I knew it, I just knew it! Why were you holding back, Teacher?"

"Kano! How many times do I have to tell you that I'm not a ghost!"

"But you said you couldn't get sunburn. That can only mean one thing."

"Yes, it means 100 SPF. I'm a big fan of sunscreen. Anyway, I think this location provides a nice backdrop so we can discuss your progress. Wouldn't you agree?"

"Uh, sure. Shall I start? Learning about Lea Salongpas— hah, only kidding—Lea Salonga. Wow, she's amazing! I heard her name brought up at Maria's house, as the titas were talking about her, but the conversation was kind of in Taglish, so it was hard to understand. But for sure, they were talking about her—seemed in a good way. She's a great ambassador for the Filipino people, isn't she?"

"She sure is."

"I was also bowled over by Nepomuceno. Get it? Bowled over? Teacher, you're not laughing."

"Actually, that wasn't bad, Kano. What else?"

"I'm still down with the aswang and usog thing, and loved hearing the story of the birth of your daughter, as well as some new superstitions."

"Is that all, Kano?"

"Not exactly. I do have something more to say."

"Really?" said the Teacher, excited. Something more?"

"Yes, it's about the adobo. I so wanted to eat some. Teacher, can you think some up for me?"

"Kano, I hope when you marry Maria… if you marry Maria… the 'something more' will be more than just a good meal."

"If I marry Maria? Yes, of course I'll want something more than dinner—a beautiful life together, filled with lots of children."

"Kano, although that's not exactly the 'something more' I'm looking for, it's a lovely sentiment. Still, not a bad day for you…. Here, you've earned another lumpia shanghai," said the Teacher, as he pulled a nice crispy one from behind his back and gave it to the Kano.

"Uh, Teacher?"

"Yes, what is it?"

Staring at the lumpia, the Kano said, "These lumpia you've been giving me…er, that I've been earning. They're never wrapped in a napkin. Or in tin foil. Or on a paper plate wrapped in tin foil. Are you sure your hands are clean, Teacher?"

"Kano, regretfully… this is very difficult."

"Why, you haven't been using hand sanitizer?"

"No, it's not that."

"Teacher, you're… you're not looking good. Or sounding good. What is it?"

"Kano, I'm sorry, but… but, I feel my connection to you beginning to fade, to weaken—because although you've made some progress, which is good and noble, your spirt is still too much kano. You have to develop your Filipino spirit if you expect to win Maria's heart. I'm not sure if you have it in you."

"Teacher, what are you saying?"

"I don't think you are ready yet," said the Teacher. "I don't know when you will be."

"Uh, okay, I mean, I thought I was ready, but if you say I'm not, then I can train more, right? As long as it takes, right? Right, Teacher?"

"Kano, I wish you had advanced further in your instruction and training, further in your 'getting it' at this point. Because I'm… I'm… I'm out of lumpia shanghai."

"Wha… wha… what are you talking about? You're out of lumpy shanghais? Well, can't you just get more? Isn't there a tindahan you can Espiritu into? This is it? We're finished? Teacher, what's going on?" asked a panicked Kano.

"Well, I can't stay with you forever, Kano. There are other vibrations in the ether that are calling out for my assistance. You say you want to get your Filipino on, but, you appear to be holding back. There just seems to be something missing in all of this… something more. Don't get me wrong: You have made some progress. You have acquired knowledge in some ways of the Filipino and developed a better appreciation for the culture, and I'm very pleased how you've taken to the food—although I'm not surprised about that. Still, my sense is you're doing this more for your gain than anything else."

"My gain?"

"Yes, you want to win Maria's heart, I don't doubt it. But, like I say, it seems like you haven't really gone all in. It's said that when you marry a Filipina, you marry her whole family. Are you really ready for that?"

"Teacher, yes, of course. I'm ready to give Maria everything."

"Everything? I'm not sure, Kano. We've been at this for a few days now, and it's the 'something more' part. I'm just not seeing it—I can't teach it either, but I'll know when I see it."

Standing on the cliffs, overlooking the wide river below, created a sense of drama the Kano could have done without. The Teacher continued. "I'm afraid this will be the last time we're together Kano. *Nais ko na rin.* I wish you well." And then, in an instant—poof! The Teacher was gone.

"Teacher, Teacher!" the Kano cried out. "Teacher!" But save for the sound of the wind blowing through the leaves of the trees below, all that could be heard was the echoing of his screams. "Teacher, Teacher," he cried out again. The Kano was alone and afraid. He sat down on the rocks, pressed his back up against a smooth boulder and closed his eyes. "Teacher, Teacher," he whispered under his breath. "Teacher, Teacher," he repeated countless times before exhaustion took over and he eventually fell asleep. He was without his Teacher—and alone.

CHAPTER 10
GOOD MOURNING

Bzz. Bzz. Bzz. 5:00 a.m. Like previous mornings, the Kano groaned and slapped at the nightstand in an attempt to stop the buzzing. But then suddenly he sat up, eyes wide, and shouted out in the darkness, "Teacher, Teacher!"

But this morning was different. There was no Teacher. The Kano's instruction and training in The Way of the Filipino had come to a sudden end yesterday. There would be no lumpia shanghai. The Kano was feeling down, but decided to put on a brave face anyway. "Fine, fine, Teacher," he said to no one in particular. "Who needs you anyway? All you've done is criticize me and tell me what I'm doing wrong. Well, things will be different now." He got out of bed, cleaned up, and made his way downstairs to the kitchen. "Hah, who needs Teacher. Time to start practicing my Filipino cooking skills so I can impress Maria."

"Kano!"

"Teacher!" The Kano couldn't hide the big smile that lit up his face, but still he remained stern. "What are you doing here? I thought yesterday was it, you know, over. Over and out. No more training. No more shanghais, right? Who do you think you are, anyway?" he demanded, his smile now a scowl. "What do you want now—Teacher?"

"Kano, aren't you happy to see me? You were crying all night long. Your subconscious mind was so strongly fixated on me, your thought vibrations so persistent, that you literally pulled me back to you, like file shavings to a magnet."

"Oh, so I'm just some leftover file shavings and you're a magnet? Who's the one with the magnetic personality here? Hello?"

"Hah, good to see you haven't lost your sense of humor, Kano."

"Uh, that wasn't a joke, Teacher. Anyway, why weren't you in my bedroom, like you've been the past several mornings, frightening me out of my sleep?"

"Remember," said the Teacher, "I am activated by your thought waves. First, you were crying out for me in your dreams, so that got my attention. Then, when you woke up, not surprisingly, you thought about food, so here we are in the kitchen, as this is where your thought waves traveled to. Haven't we gone over this before?"

"Fine, but just for the record, I wasn't crying in my sleep because… I wasn't… well, I just thought, that, you know," said the Kano as his voice began to trail into a whisper, "that you were gone."

"So you weren't crying over me? Like you do for spilled milk? Then tell me Kano, exactly why were you crying?"

"Uh, I, uh, I was dreaming of bifsteak, and had to cut a lot of onions. Yes, that's it, lots of them, so I'm sure that's why my pillow was soaked when I woke up. Or, maybe I just knocked over the glass of water near the alarm clock," said the Kano. "Nothing to do with you, okay?"

"Hmm, I might buy that story, but it's unlikely, since your thought waves of me in your sleep were seriously intense. Nonetheless, it's true, I have returned, but—you are still not fully transformed in The Way of the Filipino. You understand that, right? I can give you just one more chance, but that's going to be it, Kano. You either are transformed, or you're not. It's that simple."

"Teacher, I'll do anything. *Anything.* Even eat some babaloot. Right now."

"Babaloot? You sound like Ricky Ricardo. It's balut, not babaloot! See, you should know that by now. Okay, let's put that behind us. You were thinking of cooking up some Filipinos this morning? Uh, I mean cooking up some Filipino food, is that right?"

"Yes, I want to impress Maria with my cooking skills, so I'm going to make—"

"Reservations," interrupted the Teacher. "I suggest you make reservations at a nice restaurant. Let's not leave things up to chance at this point."

"Teacher, I'm trying to get my Filipino on, and you're discouraging me."

"When it comes to the food thing, you don't need to be the next Chef Comerford to be authentic. If you're interested in learning how to cook Filipino for Maria, that's great, and I'm sure she'll appreciate it. But a better approach is to simply start by eating the foods of her culture with an open mind along with an open mouth. Believe me, that will help you far more in your transformation," said the Teacher.

"Fine," said the Kano. "But I'm serious about this. I want to wear one of those paper chef hats, too."

"Kano, your instruction and training over the last few days has been at some nice venues—a wedding, a child's birthday party, and the Mendoza's home, where we heard some lively Filipino conversations."

"Yes, I've really enjoyed it, and I can't wait to tell Maria all I've learned."

"Kano, you can't actually tell her what's happened—I mean, you can't tell her about me, and thought waves, and Septem-bah—she'll think you're loko-loko," said the Teacher.

"Teacher, is *loko-loko* spelled with two *c*'s or two *k*'s?

"*K* as in *kano*. Anyway, what I'm saying is that you go back to Maria with a new spirit of appreciation and love of the Filipino culture, by how you act and what you do, not by a pronouncement. Actions speak louder than words."

"Actions speak louder than words—check," said the Kano. "So, what will you be teaching me today, Teacher?"

"The circle of life. Today we'll be observing what happens with the passing of a loved one."

"Uh, I'm not sure I want to see that," said the Kano gravely.

"That's understandable, but the beauty of such an occasion," said the Teacher, "if I can describe it in that way, is the outpouring of love. Yes, there's sadness and crying and grief, but also moments of levity and laughter, and the reuniting of relatives and loved ones."

"Okay, then, I think I'm ready, Teacher," said the Kano.

"Ang Aking Espiritu Ay Filipino," said the Teacher while the Kano held onto him. "Ang aking Espiritu Ay Filipino. Ang Aking Espiritu Ay Filipino." In a flash, they were at a funeral home.

"What can you tell me about Filipino funerals?" asked the Kano.

"Well, as you can see, we've been transported to a wake. In the Philippines, the wake is known as a *lamay* or *paglalamay* and usually lasts a few days longer than it does in the US. The mourners provide some financial assistance, called *abuloy*, to help the family of the deceased with funeral costs."

"That's a nice gesture," said the Kano.

"It is. For Catholics, there's a custom called *pasiyam* or *pagsisiyam* where mourners pray the rosary for the deceased for nine days."

"What does pasiyam mean?" asked the Kano.

"It means 'to do for nine days,' as there's a folk belief that the soul of the departed enters into the afterlife on the ninth day," said the Teacher. "Then, on the 40th day, there's a special prayer service, or even a mass, as a reminder of the 40 days between Christ's Resurrection and Ascension. On the first anniversary of the passing, another remembrance service is held. This is called *babang luksâ*."

"It all sounds very nice... and comforting," said the Kano.

Just then, the Lola came to the sitting room in the back of the funeral home, where the Teacher and Kano had been transported. The room was full of an assortment of Filipino foods and beverages, including beer for the men. Lola was accompanied by a few of the younger children, and they all sat down. The children began picking at some of the desserts and looked toward the Lola, as she told them she had something to say.

"Children, you must be very careful not to sneeze in front of the dead person," she said.

"Why, Lola?" they all asked in unison.

"Because you will also die."

"Aah!" screamed the children.

"And, children, do not let your parents take you home directly after the funeral."

"Why, Lola?" they asked.

"Because the spirit of the dead person will follow you home."

"Aah!" screamed the children.

"And, children, don't place your hands on top of your heads."

"Why not, Lola?"

"Because one of your parents might die," she said.

"Aah!" screamed the children.

"And children, remember, if you are dreaming and a dead person asks you to come along with him, don't go!"

"Aah!" screamed the children.

Hearing the commotion, Floribeth, the Lola's daughter, ran to the back room to see what was happening. "Ma, what's going on?"

"Just passing some good old fashion advice on to the next generation," she said.

"Well, I'm not sure how good it is. The children sound frightened."

"It's okay, Tita, we're not scared," said a little one. "Well, maybe just a little, but we love Lola and know she wants to teach us about some traditions and even superstitions about our culture."

"See," said the Lola.

"Okay, children, but know it's all in good fun," said Floribeth as she walked out toward the viewing room. Lola called the children over. "Anak," she whispered. "Anak."

"Hmm, is that a knock? Is there a knock at the door?" asked the Kano. "Or is the knock coming from the coffin? Teacher, is the dead knocking on his own coffin! Aah!"

"Shh!" said the Teacher. "Anak means 'children.' Remember? I pointed that out earlier in your training. She is calling the children over to her."

"Uh, yes, that's right—I mean, I remember."

"Anak," continued the Lola, "A few more things. Don't take any of the food from this wake back to your home."

"Why, Lola?" they asked.

"Let me guess," the Kano said to himself. "It will bring bad luck."

"It will bring bad luck," said the Lola. "Who of you has eaten rice here today?"

"We all have, Lola," they said, "We're Filipino!"

"Did you eat all of it? Did you leave not even one grain of rice on the plate?"

"Well, I think we ate most of it, maybe just a little left on our plates," one of the children said. "Why?"

"Because the number of rice grains left on your plate signifies the number of days you'll spend in purgatory."

"Uy," they all said.

"But, it's good to eat at a wake when the deceased is old, like today, because you will gain the person's luck of living into old age."

"Is there anything else we should know, Lola?"

"Yes, do not dream of losing a tooth."

"Why?"

"It means that someone in the family might be dying. Also, for those of you with little baby brothers and sisters, make sure your mother dresses them in bright red."

"Why red?" asked the children.

"So that the spirit of the dead does not appear to your little brother or sister."

"Aah!" screamed the children.

"Shh," said Lola. "Or your tita will come back here." Cupping her one hand and moving it as if she were doing a doggie paddle, she motioned to a few children by the table. "You three, by the table, come here; don't stand so close to each other."

"Why not, Lola?" they asked.

"Because when you form groups of three or thirteen, one of you will die."

"Aah!"

"Ma, what are you doing?" asked Floribeth gently as she made her way back into the room. "Children, go play with your cousin Bhoy, he brought some yo-yos."

"Teacher, is that a Filipino custom? Bringing yo-yos to a wake? To signify the ups and downs of life?"

"No, it's not. I guess their cousin just brought yo-yos because he likes to play with them. And it's more fun to have a few people yo-yo-ing together."

"I guess yo. I mean so. I guess so."

"Did you know that the yo-yo was invented by a Filipino, a Mr. Pedro Flores?"

"Seriously? The yo-yo is a Filipino thing?" asked the Kano.

"Yes," said the Teacher. "At least as we know it today. Although, Flores, being the humble man he was, did not claim to be the inventor."

"You say he was the inventor, but he said he wasn't? Which is it, Teacher?"

"Flores was proud of his Filipino heritage and culture. He never claimed to be the inventor, suggesting instead that his yo-yo creation was inspired by a Filipino combat weapon used 400 years ago against the Spaniards and other intruders."

"A combat weapon? No wonder my brother bruised so easily when my yo-yo hit him in the head during the 'around the world' trick."

"Yes, it was a large weapon, with sharp edges and studs and attached to a thick 20 foot rope for flinging at enemies or prey," said the Teacher.

"Ouch!"

"There's some evidence that forms of the yo-yo originated in 1,000 BC in China and 500 BC in Greece.

Toys similar in design were in the US in the 1860s, but they never truly achieved fad status until Flores began mass-producing them."

Did You Know?
That the inventor of the yo-yo was Pedro Flores,
a Filipino immigrant to the U.S.

"So interesting, Teacher. Is *yo-yo* a Tagalog word?"

"My understanding is that it derives from an Ilocano word meaning 'come-back' or 'come-come.'"

"Cool-cool."

"Flores is the iconic American 'rags to riches' story. He came to this country as an immigrant in 1915, with nothing, and soon began his yo-yo company in Santa Barbara, California. He started with a dozen yo-yos, all handmade, and 18 months later he had three factories producing 300,000 yo-yos a day and employing 600 workers! In 1932 he sold his company to an American businessman named Donald F. Duncan, who began manufacturing under the Duncan Yo-Yo name we know today. The rest, as they say, is history."

"Floribeth," said the Lola as the children scampered away, "it's important that the next generation know these things. You may dismiss them as just old crazy folklore. Maybe you're right, but maybe you're wrong. That's why I say 'bahala na.'"

"There's that bahala na again," said the Kano.

"Yes, remember, it roughly translates to 'come what may,'" said the Teacher.

"By the way," asked the Lola, "why is the deceased wearing shoes?"

"Uh, I'm not, uh… why are you asking that, Ma?"

"You need to take them off him."

"Take them off? What are you talking about?"

"The dead shouldn't be wearing shoes. A dead person who is buried with his shoes on will haunt his relatives, and when he arrives, his loud footsteps will be heard."

"Ma, please."

"And, make sure his rosary is cut into pieces before burial," said the Lola.

"This is a new one to me," said her daughter. "Why cut up a perfectly good string of rosary beads?"

"Because if the rosary is cut into pieces, it will prevent further tragedy from falling upon the family."

"I think we'll leave the rosary beads just as they are."

"Suit yourself. By the way, are the deceased's palms open or closed?"

"I'm not really sure. What do you mean, open or closed?"

"His fists. Are her fists clenched, or are they open?" asked the Lola.

"I think they're closed. Why?"

"Hmm, maybe you should pry them open," suggested the Lola.

"Pry them open?" Floribeth asked, a bit confused.

"Yes, because if they're closed, his family will have trouble with money. But when the dead's palms are open, the family won't have any financial difficulties."

"I'm not going to rearrange the body, Ma."

Looking at the assortment of food throughout the room, the Lola asked, "Why is there pansit here?"

"Because our visitors will be hungry. I'm surprised you're asking about that, Ma. You're the queen of worrying that there isn't enough food for the guests."

"Yes, having more than enough food for one's guest is a sign of a Filipino's hospitality, but at a wake, you must be careful that it's the right food."

"The right food? What does that mean?"

"Everything here is fine… except for the pancit."

"Ma, please, I know my pancit isn't as good as Tito Angel's, but his adobo isn't as good as mine."

"No, that's not it. Pancit should not be served at the wake because it will lengthen the mourning period," said the Lola.

"Long noodle thing?"

"Yes, that's right. But eating pancit after the funeral will lengthen the lives of the relatives," said the Lola as she put aluminum foil over the tray of pancit and hid it out of sight.

"Is it warm in here?" asked Floribeth.

"No, why do you ask?"

"I'm feeling a bit… warm. Can you move over? I'll sit down on the couch with you."

"Do you have a fever?" asked the Lola, putting her cheek on her daughter's forehead.

"Why, afraid you'll catch something?"

"Not me," said the Lola, "I'm not afraid. But if you're catching a fever, it means the deceased spirit is trying to remind you of an unfulfilled obligation to him. Do you owe her some money?"

"Ma, please, let me just rest a minute. It's been a trying day."

"I'm glad the deceased didn't die like your cousin Jojo," said the Lola.

"Jojo? I don't remember him."

"You were very young. Jojo was tragically killed by some bad men. So sad."

"Was the culprit caught?"

"Yes, those chicks got him!" said the Lola.

"Chicks? Do you mean female police officers? Ma, I think we should be more respectful and just call them police officers."

"No, I mean chicks," said the Lola. "You know, chirp-chirp."

"Chirp-chirp? Ma, I'm sorry, I don't understand what you're trying to say."

"When the cause of death is murder, you are supposed to place chicks in the coffin," said the Lola.

"Why?"

"Doing so will bring the murderer to justice because the chicks symbolize eating away at the murderer's conscience."

"And... and you put live chickens in Jojo's coffin?"

"Not chickens, baby chicks!"

"Exactly how was the culprit brought to justice?" asked Floribeth.

"She just turned himself in," said the Lola. "Guilt. His conscience was eaten away."

"Ma, some things are just coincidences."

"Was it a coincidence last summer when a black butterfly entered the Rodriquez's home... and Rowena died the next day?"

"Ma, Rowena was their dog!" said Floribeth. "And she was 16 years old!"

"Bahala na," said the Lola. "And, was it a coincidence when your tito's cousin's mother's son's wife's nephew Danilo dreamed of riding in a boat... and the next day, when he was riding in a boat, fell out of it?"

"Ma, Danilo didn't meet a bad omen with that dream. He's was just a boy. Sadly, he went on a badly maintained boat ride at the local carnival. The door didn't lock, and he fell out of it," said the daughter.

" Bahala na," said the Lola.

"And what about your superstition about planting a tree upon the birth of a child? Hmm? You know the one that says the child will die?" You remember our neighbors, Mr. and Mrs. Ocampo? They had14 children, and they planted a tree with each child's birth. No one died, Ma."

"Bahala na," said the Lola once more.

"And how many times have you told me that when my dog Fido is barking at me, it signifies my impending death, just because he's barking? Ma, dogs do that you know, they bark! And don't 'bahala na' me again."

"Okay, I won't say 'bahala na,' I'll just think it."

"Uy," said her daughter as she left the room.

"Teacher," asked the Kano, "are there other things regarding wakes, funerals, or the passing of a loved one that I should know about?"

"Yes, the passing over the grave," said the Teacher.

"Passing over the grave? What do you mean?"

"When my father-in-law Juan was buried—and a real good man, father and provider, by the way—we passed our daughter, who happened to be the youngest granddaughter at the time, over his grave. Basically, it's a handing of the child from one person to another, over the burial site," said the Teacher.

"What's the significance?" asked the Kano.

"It's done so the ghost of the dead won't visit the child. Also, it can symbolize burying the child's sickness along with the dead," said the Teacher.

"Like a lot of Filipino customs and superstitions, is that done just to do it… I mean, something passed down, without really believing it?" asked the Kano.

"Yes, that may be true, it's not like everybody believes in all of these things, but—"

"But what?" asked the Kano.

"Bahala na" said the Teacher, "Bahala na."

CHAPTER 11
HOLD ONTO YOUR NOSES

"Hah," said the Kano to the alarm clock. "You don't wake me up, I turn you off!"

It was 4:58 a.m., two minutes before his Teacher-imposed 5 a.m. reveille. This time, it was he who would say good morning first—but the teacher wasn't anywhere in sight. "Teacher, good morning. Where are you? Olly olly oxen free."

He went downstairs to look for him in the kitchen. Sure enough, that's where he was, writing on the flip chart.

"Kano, I just poured your coffee; it's on the table. Please, sit down."

"'*Bisperas ng Bagong Taon*'?" asked the Kano, looking at the flip chart as he grabbed the cup and sat down.

"Yes, that's right," said the Teacher. "I thought it might be nice to spend New Year's Eve, or as we say in Tagalog, 'Bisperas ng Bagong Taon,' with the Mendozas."

The Kano started to laugh. "New Year's? Teacher, it's still summer. Are you telling me that Filipinos have a New Year's Eve in July kind of thing?"

"Kano, remember, you're dealing with my Filipino spirit. I'm not bound by time or space. If we want to go to a Filipino New Year's celebration, we just need to summon our inner Filipino."

"Uh-oh, do you mean we're going to Remem-bah right now?" asked the Kano. "I don't think I'm dressed up enough for New Year's Eve—seeing I'm still in my pajamas and all."

"Don't worry, no need to Remem-bah right now, Kano, because later, we'll be in a house full of New Year's partying, karaoke-singing Filipinos. If there's any 21st night of Septem-bah stuff going on, it won't have anything to do with me!"

"Phew."

"Some background on the holiday is in order," said the Teacher as he joined the Kano at the table. "As I mentioned, in Tagalog we call New Year's Eve 'Bisperas ng Bagong Taon,' and shouting '*Manigong Bagong Taon!*' is the equivalent of saying 'Happy New Year!'"

"I'd better stick with the equivalent."

"Like so much in the Filipino culture, it's a time for family... and for food! It's a tradition of Filipinos to put as much food on the table as possible for the *Media Noche*, a lavish midnight feast, because it is believed to bring prosperity for the whole year."

"More food? Count me in!" said the Kano. "Except for the chocolate pudding."

"If you let Maria know you are looking forward to the New Year's Eve feast, you might get some brownie points. Or, should I say, some sticky rice points."

"Sticky rice points?" asked the Kano.

"Yes, sticky rice, or *malagkit*, is served on New Year's Eve, because it symbolizes family togetherness," said the Teacher. "An added benefit is that it's believed that good luck will stick to you throughout the year. Pansit noodles are served to represent a long life, and eggs are eaten as a symbol of new life. *Pinoy kakanin* symbolize closeness and unity within the family."

"I'm getting hungry," said the Kano.

"I'm not surprised," said the Teacher. "Let's not forget about shrimp. Most Filipinos love shrimp… but there are mixed opinions about serving shrimps during New Year's and—"

Interrupting, the Kano said, "Teacher, the plural of shrimp is *shrimp*, not shrimps. Leave off the last 's' for plural."

"Kano, remember. Little subtleties of the language, like saying 'shrimps' with an 's,' are to be appreciated, and enjoyed. Remember, as well as English is spoken by most Filipinos, it's not their native tongue. Anyway, there's some belief that it's bad luck to serve shrimps on New Year's Eve because shrimps are known as bottom dwellers, while others believe that shrimps or prawns stand for prosperity and good health," said the Teacher.

"I actually do love shrimp," said the Kano. "And I'm not a bottom dweller. Except when I lived in my parent's basement for a couple of years, but that's another story."

"It's good to serve sweet-tasting food. The sweetness of the food stands for a rich and sweet life," said the Teacher. "Conversely, you should avoid serving bitter-tasting food. Eating bitter food creates a scowl on your face. You wouldn't want to welcome the New Year with a frown!"

"Wow, I never knew food could be so complicated," said the Kano.

"It's not the food that's complicated," suggested the Teacher, with a little scowl of his own.

"How about the fish with the googley eyes?"

"There will be fish, and on New Year's Eve, it takes on some meaning."

"What do you mean?"

"It's a custom borrowed from the Chinese. In Mandarin, fish are called *yu,* which means 'excess' or 'surplus.' So, it means that to have fish, one will have more than enough in the new year."

"Sounds kind of fishy to me."

"And the fish with the eyes," said the Teacher, "when it's served whole like that, it's supposed to symbolize a good beginning and a good ending for the coming year."

"What if chicken is served? Does it mean you're going to be afraid all next year? Get it? A chicken?" said the Kano as he flapped his arms like wings and clucked and strutted around the room.

"Kano! If you're serious about winning the heart of the fabulous Filipina, you need to stop acting like a chicken and get your ducks in a row," said the Teacher with a completely straight face.

"You're right, ducks in a row, check," said the Kano.

"Now, regarding chicken, some families won't serve it on New Year's Eve to avoid any financial problems."

"Financial problems? Wasn't, like, 100 years ago in America, having a chicken in your pot was supposed to be a sign of prosperity?" asked the Kano.

"The Republican party promised that to the voters in 1928 if Herbert Hoover was elected. But getting back to our discussion, the chicken can be associated with the Filipino saying, '*isang kahig, isang tuka*,' which has some connection to poverty and hardship. It roughly translates to 'one scratch, one peck,' or a poor, hand-to-mouth existence— kind of like living paycheck to paycheck. I've also heard it wise to just avoid anything with wings, so your finances or livelihood won't fly away. How about fruit; you like fruit, don't you?" asked the Teacher.

"Sure."

"You'll see lots of fruit. On New Year's, the meal is served with 12 different sweet fruits, where each signifies a month; and, they are all round shaped, which is considered to bring luck and fortune to all. This tradition apparently has its origins from the Chinese," said the Teacher.

"Gotcha," said the Kano. "Any other sayings or superstitions for New Year's?"

"Wear polka dots."

"Polka dots… you mean, like Minnie Mouse red dress white polka dots kind of polka dots?" asked the Kano.

"Don't ruin Disney for me," said the Teacher. "For you, maybe just some polka-dot socks. But don't be surprised if you see Maria wearing a polka dot blouse or dress, as round shapes signify prosperity and happiness. Or she may be wearing red, because the color red is for good luck. This too comes from the Chinese. Maybe she'll be wearing both red and polka dots. Hmm, maybe you've got a point about Minnie Mouse."

"Are there some other interesting things about Filipinos and New Year's?" asked the Kano.

"Here's an interesting one, but I'm not sure how closely it's followed by my asawa."

"And what is that, Teacher?"

"In the Philippines, it is strictly forbidden to spend money on the first day of the New Year. It is believed that spending on New Year's Day would mean losing money for the whole of the coming year. Yes, now that I think of it, I wish my wife would get her Filipina on for that one!"

"What else happens, or doesn't happen?" asked the Kano.

"Houses are cleaned spic and span. But curiously, once the clock strikes midnight, you must avoid sweeping altogether."

"What, no walis tambo?" said the Kano.

"Yes, that's right," said the Teacher. "Avoid sweeping the floor after midnight because you might drive away the good luck that just entered the home."

"Why am I not surprised by that one?" said the Kano. "What else should I know?"

The Teacher continued. "To ensure that you do not go hungry in the coming year, fill the rice bin to the brim. Same goes with the salt and sugar containers. If you have a water reservoir, fill it too. Keep it full until after the first day of the New Year."

"No walis tambo-ing, no spending money, fill the bins and jugs to the top. Check." said the Kano.

"Since Maria lives here in the New Jersey area, it will be wintertime and cold on New Year's Eve. I suggest you dress warmly," said the Teacher.

"Why? We're not celebrating outdoors."

"That may be true, but, don't be surprised if Maria keeps some windows open… maybe even a door open, until midnight."

"This has something to do with good luck?" asked the Kano proudly.

"Yes, so that good fortune can enter and evil can exit. Another way to welcome good luck into your home is to open all the lights inside the house before midnight," said the Teacher.

"'Open the lights'? Do you mean expose the bulbs or something? Take off the lamp shades?" asked the Kano.

"My apologies, Kano. It's my Filipino spirit. Not 'open,' 'turn on.' Turn on the lights. You'll hear Filipinos often say 'open the lights' vs. 'turn on the lights.'"

"I can't say 'open the lights' or 'turn on the lights' in the Tagalog language, Teacher, so I'm starting to appreciate that most Filipinos can speak multiple languages."

"I'm pleased to hear you say that, Kano."

"Teacher, didn't you say that you had a story to tell about your own Filipino New Year's Eve?"

"Yes. I'll never forget my first New Year's Eve with my asawa, who at the time was my girlfriend. We had been dating for just a few months, and she invited me over to celebrate New Year's Eve with her family."

"Yes, go on."

"She didn't explain anything to me—the food, lights, windows... over time, just by being married, these traditions sort of unfolded. But that night, I noticed as midnight approached, an excitement build. That's not exclusive to Filipinos on New Year's Eve, of course, but there was an energy level I really picked up on. And the noise."

"The noise?" asked the Kano.

"Yes, there was great interest in making noise. I remember my sister-in-law Marites to be the most loko-

loko, or crazy, and I mean that in a good, celebratory way. She was using multiple noise makers and screaming quite alarmingly."

"Does making lots of noise have something to do with driving out evil spirits?" asked the Kano.

"Exactly. You want to drive away all evil spirits from your life and create space for good ones," said the Teacher.

"Then what happened?"

"The excitement and noise reached a fever pitch... and then at midnight I saw something I will never forget. I was simply not prepared," said the Teacher.

"What... what was it, Teacher?" asked the Kano.

"Exactly at midnight, everyone starting jumping up and down and pulling on their noses!"

"What?"

"Yes, jumping and laughing and pulling on their noses, shouting Manigong Bagong Taon! or 'Happy New Year!' Oh, and the coins. Coins seemed to be showering down from everywhere, hitting the ceiling or scattering across the floor and making lots of noise, and everybody was screaming," said the Teacher. "It was crazy!"

"Did you say coins?" asked the Kano. "A shower of coins?"

"Yes, it's the money shower. The lolos and lolas, and titos and titas are secretly hiding bags or pocketsful of coins, then shouting 'Happy New Year!' while throwing handful after handful of coins for the children to grab and keep for themselves. You might even find an adult scrambling for some on occasion! The belief is that by doing this, money will continuously flow into the house in the New Year. Money in your pocket means money all year around. Although the coins are considered lucky and therefore shouldn't be spent, they always are. My children always anticipated what they could buy with the lucky fortunes they received on New Year's Eve."

"Wow, that sounds exciting. I can understand the connection between coins and prosperity... but I'm still confused by the jumping up and down and the pulling of noses," said the Kano.

"The idea is that if you jump at midnight, you will become taller, so it's especially important that children do it," said the Teacher. "And the pulling on the nose is to make it straighter—more European-like, and less flat. But like I told you before, I love the Filipino nose just as it is!"

"Does anyone really believe they'll become taller or have a straighter nose?" asked the Kano.

"No, no one really believes it. But I must tell you, it makes New Year's Eve a lot of pun... I mean fun!" Now, get ready and hold onto your nose Kano—we're off to the Mendozas' to bring in the New Year!"

CHAPTER 12
MANNY PO

"Teacher?" asked the Kano, with equal parts of surprise and curiosity in his voice. "Are we standing on the beach? Right now? I thought you'd let me sleep in after our New Year's par-tay. Don't you have to teach me something before we have our beach-bro moment? Uh, Teacher, you look serious. What's going on?"

Manny Pacquiao

"Kano, it's time."

"It's time?"

"Yes, it's time," said the Teacher.

"Gulp."

The Teacher extended his right arm towards the Kano, palm up, fist closed. "Look at my hand."

The Kano's eyes were fixated as the Teacher slowly uncurled his fingers, exposing something in his hand—it appeared to be a fried food, light brown in color and tubular in shape. Curiously, the sound of a flute started to permeate the air, similar to that in a Chinese martial arts film, as the student learns from the master.

"Teacher, this feels strangely familiar. Didn't we start out like this—you know, the lumpy Chinese thing with the music and all?"

"Kano," began the Teacher, "When *you* can take *this* lumpia shanghai from my hand, it will be time for you to mano-po."

Instinctively, the Kano took the lumpia shanghai from the Teacher's hand, holding it between his index finger and thumb. He stared at it momentarily, and then bit into it. *Crunch.* It tasted different than before. He bit into it once more. *Crunch.* Yes, this was very different. As he swallowed the last morsel, a strange feeling came over him, and before his mind's eye a scene instantly flashed by. In a jungle clearing, he saw a solitary balut egg, lying on the ground. It started to rock back and forth, back and forth, and suddenly cracked open, hatching the Kano himself, but not as himself exactly—he was a baby mallard duckling! He waddled right, and waddled left, shook the remaining shell fragments off his tail feathers, and swiftly took flight, high above the Philippine islands, all 7,000 of them. He saw the breathtaking unspoiled beauty of the country, the turquoise crystal-clear waters, and tropical lush forests; he saw the white sandy beaches of Boracay; vast plantations of mouth-watering pineapples in Mindanao; the Banaue Rice terraces; caves, lakes, and waterfalls; he saw the Chocolate Hills in Bohol and the green rice fields in Tibiao; colorful Jeepneys; churches, chapels, and statues of Jesus and Mary; he saw the Baroque churches, and well-preserved Spanish-era mansions in Vigay; he saw the mighty Mayon volcano and the tiny Taal, birds of all species and fascinating reptiles; spectacular views of landscapes, villages, and rivers; he saw lively and vibrant festivals—*Sinulog* in Cebu, *Dinagyang* in Iloilo City, and the *Ati-Atihan* in Aklan, among so many.

But even more magnificent than this beautiful tropical paradise called the Philippines were the Filipino people themselves.

He flew closer to the ground and passed by Filipinos, millions of Filipinos, who were looking up, waving to him, and smiling… smiling that big, beautiful, joyful smile that is so wonderfully and distinctly Filipino.

He saw so much, so quickly. He saw the Manilamen— truly, the first overseas Filipino workers—who escaped the harsh life on the Spanish galleons to form the earliest

Filipino settlement in the US, in the marshlands of Louisiana, in the 1700s. And they were smiling.

He saw the pensionados, scholars who traded the comforts of a middle class life in the Philippines for the prospect a better education in America. And they were smiling.

He saw families, and children. Beautiful, angelic children. And lolos and lolas. All over the Philippines he saw them. Praying in church and studying in school; he saw them celebrating at weddings and grieving at funerals. He saw girls dancing the *pandanggo sa ilaw* and boys playing basketball. He saw them rich and he saw them poor. And they were smiling.

He saw the devastation of Typhoon Yolanda and other natural disasters, and how soon after the damage was done, children would find an empty can, a flip-flop, or a stick and start playing again, and having fun. He saw ancient invasions of the islands and the fighting spirit of Filipino soldiers in World War II. He saw balikbayan boxes, the heroism of Jose Rizal, and the heart of Carlos Bulosan. He saw the hardships of martial law and the hope of the People's Power Revolution. Through it all, he saw the Filipino people smiling.

He saw Filipino men leave behind their family and loved ones, a long time ago that was not so long ago, full of hope for a new life in America, only to become a cheap migrating labor supply for Hawaii plantations, California farms, and the Alaska fishing industry. But in their hardship they opened the door for the generations of Filipinos who would follow—who would find a good life in America. And so they smiled.

And now, he knew why Filipinos smiled that big, beautiful, joyful smile. It was *kasiyahan*, that special state of joy, borne from the resilience of the Filipino heart, or *hindi natitinag ang pusong Pilipino*. Yes, he now understood the 'something more' the Teacher had been waiting to see, and what the Kano had needed to discover. The Kano opened his eyes. The time to mano-po was upon them. He intuitively knew what to do. "Teacher, I'm going to miss you."

"Yes, I know."

The Kano waited, somewhat expectantly, but the Teacher did not say anything back. "Teacher, I'm going to miss you," he repeated. Nothing. "That's it? You're not going to say it back? Won't you miss me too?"

The Teacher just smiled.

The Kano reached for the Teacher's right hand, bowed slightly and touched his forehead to the back of his hand, in a perfect mano-po.

"How's that for a mano-manny- pack eey ow?" asked the Kano, looking up to the Teacher.

"You have my blessing, Kano. *Ikaw ay isang Pilipino sa espiritu*. You are now a Filipino in spirit. You have proven yourself worthy of Maria." Poof! In an instant, he was gone.

"Teacher, Teacher!" shouted the Kano. It was useless— he would never see the Teacher again. Standing on the shoreline, he looked out on the distant horizon as the tide rolled rhythmically in and out—and heard something. It was the sound of music, at first so faint it required the Kano to strain to hear it. But the volume grew stronger until the melody seemed to fill the beach. The Kano was pleased. It was a familiar refrain and a parting gift from the Teacher—it was "Do You Remem-bah."

"Do I Remem-bah?" the Kano asked as he stood alone on the beach. "I'll never forget," he smiled. "The 21st night of Septem-bah, Teacher. The 21st night of Septem-bah."

Wakas
(The End)

BIBLIOGRAPHY

Andres, Thomas D, and Pilar B. Ilada-Andres. *Understanding the Filipino*. Quezon City, Philippines: New Day Publishers, 1987.

Luning, Bonifacio Ira. *Guidebook to the Filipino Wedding*. Manila, Philippines: Vera-Reyes, Inc., 1990.

Roces, Alfredo, and Grace Roces. *Culture Shock! Philippines. A Guide to Customs and Etiquette*. Portland, OR: Graphic Arts Center Publishing Company, 1985.

Romana-Cruz, Neni Sta. *Don't Take a Bath on a Friday: Philippine Superstitions and Folk Beliefs*. Manila, Philippines: Tanahan Books, 1996.

Romana-Cruz, Neni Sta. *You Know You're a Filipino if... A Pinoy Primer*. Manila, Philippines: Tanahan Books, 1997.

Snyder, Gail. *Filipino Americans*. Philadelphia, PA: Mason Crest Publishers, 2009.

Takaki, Ronald. *In the Heart of Filipino America: Immigrants from the Pacific Isles*. New York, NY: Chelsea House Publishers, 1995.

Zabala, Larry V., Jr. *Filipinos: The Probationary Americans*. N.p.: n.p., 2017, 2012.

ABOUT THE AUTHOR

Christopher Holl may not be Filipino by birthright, but he is in spirit, as evidenced by 28 years of marriage to his Filipina wife and their "Fil-Am" children. He's fond of saying that he loves the Filipino people so much, he made four of his own!

He's a business executive, author, and former US Marine, and is eternally indebted to the unforeseen "Filipino twist of fate" that forever changed the course, and meaning, of his life.

www.ingramcontent.com/pod-product-compliance
Lightning Source LLC
Chambersburg PA
CBHW070317260626
47160CB00003B/866